BACHELOR UNFORGIVING

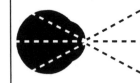

This Large Print Book carries the
Seal of Approval of N.A.V.H.

BACHELOR UNFORGIVING

BRENDA JACKSON

THORNDIKE PRESS

A part of Gale, Cengage Learning

GALE
CENGAGE Learning·

Farmington Hills, Mich • San Francisco • New York • Waterville, Maine
Meriden, Conn • Mason, Ohio • Chicago

GALE
CENGAGE Learning

Copyright © 2016 by Brenda Streater Jackson.
Thorndike Press, a part of Gale, Cengage Learning.

ALL RIGHTS RESERVED
This is a work of fiction. Names, characters, places, and incidents either are the product of the author's imagination or are used fictitiously, and any resemblance to actual persons, living or dead, business establishments, events, or locales is entirely coincidental.
Thorndike Press® Large Print African-American.
The text of this Large Print edition is unabridged.
Other aspects of the book may vary from the original edition.
Set in 16 pt. Plantin.

LIBRARY OF CONGRESS CATALOGING-IN-PUBLICATION DATA

Names: Jackson, Brenda (Brenda Streater), author.
Title: Bachelor unforgiving / by Brenda Jackson.
Description: Large print edition. | Waterville, Maine : Thorndike Press, 2016. |
    Series: Thorndike Press large print African-American
Identifiers: LCCN 2016028844 | ISBN 9781410491428 (hardcover) | ISBN 1410491420
    (hardcover)
Subjects: LCSH: African Americans—Fiction. | Large type books. | GSAFD: Love
    stories.
Classification: LCC PS3560.A21165 B29 2016 | DDC 813/.54—dc23
LC record available at https://lccn.loc.gov/2016028844

Published in 2016 by arrangement with Harlequin Books S.A.

Printed in Mexico
1 2 3 4 5 6 7 20 19 18 17 16

Dear Reader,

I'm so glad to bring another Bachelors in Demand novel to you. We've already seen four bachelors happily married off, and now there are only two remaining.

I guess you can say that I saved the best two for last . . .

Bachelor Unforgiving's hero is Virgil Bougard. There is nothing worse than an affair that goes bad. Especially when a trust factor is involved, it could make things even worse. Kara Goshay finds out the hard way that when it comes to making a mistake, some men can be unforgiving . . . like Virgil. However, Kara is convinced that love can hide a multitude of faults, and one should be forgiven for their mistakes. The problem is trying to convince Virgil of that.

I hope all of you enjoy reading Virgil and Kara's story.

Happy Reading!

Brenda Jackson

"Do not judge, and you will not be judged.
Do not condemn, and you will not be condemned.
Forgive, and you will be forgiven."
— *Luke* 6:37 NIV

ACKNOWLEDGMENTS

To the man who will always and forever be the love of my life, Gerald Jackson, Sr. To all my readers who have waited patiently for another Bachelors in Demand novel, this one is for you.

PROLOGUE

Kara Goshay knew she couldn't put it off any longer. After all, the main reason she'd attended tonight's event was to seek out Virgil Bougard. She owed him an apology and she intended to give it to him. Nothing would stop her. Not even the cold, hard glares he'd given her all evening.

She had no illusions about not being one of his favorite people. Four years ago while they had been in an exclusive affair she had accused him of doing something she now knew he hadn't done. She was woman enough to admit when she'd made a mistake, and in this case, she had made a big one.

She drew in a deep breath as she watched him. He was standing in a group, talking to five other men. She knew them. They were his godbrothers. Virgil had told her the story of how, close to forty years ago, six guys had become best friends while attending

Morehouse and on graduation day had made a pact to stay in touch by becoming godfathers to each other's children, and that the firstborn sons' names would start with the letters *U* through *Z*. And that was how Uriel Lassiter, Virgil Bougard, Winston Coltrane, Xavier Kane, York Ellis and Zion Blackstone had come to have their names.

She eyed the group of men. All six were extremely handsome, but there was something about Virgil that had captured her from the first moment they had met. He'd walked into the room at a charity event, much like this one, looking as if he'd strolled right off the cover of *GQ*. She was convinced every woman at the black-tie affair that night had done a double take and concluded that no man could be that gorgeous.

Later that night, when he'd approached her and asked her to dance, she'd gotten a close-up view, and she discovered that she was wrong. He had been *that* gorgeous. Standing over six-three with a muscular build that would make any woman's mouth water, Virgil Bougard gave greater meaning to the phrase *tall, dark and handsome*.

She continued to watch Virgil interact with his godbrothers. When he wasn't sending hard stares her way, he was smiling at something one of them said. He and his godbrothers were close, and no doubt he'd told them what she had accused him of doing. However, she appreciated that, whenever her path crossed any of theirs, they were always pleasant.

Virgil had come to the party tonight alone. And as if he still had radar where she was concerned, his gaze had unerringly found her when he had entered the ballroom. If looks could kill, she wouldn't have any life in her body right now.

Drawing in a courageous breath, she placed her wineglass on the tray of a passing waiter. Straightening her spine, she crossed the room to where Virgil stood. She would take her chances and ask to speak with him privately. She hoped that, although he felt nothing but loathing for her, he would grant her that request.

As if he sensed her impending approach, Virgil glanced her way. The blatant animosity she saw in his eyes nearly made her weak in the knees. The only thing that kept her moving forward was knowing any anger he felt toward her was justified.

Two of his godbrothers also noticed her approach. She saw a warning flash in Xavier's eyes, giving her a heads-up that to tangle with Virgil tonight wasn't a good idea, that maybe she should turn around and head the other way.

The look she saw in Uriel's gaze was unreadable. She figured he was curious as to how she could summon the nerve to come within ten feet of Virgil, given his propensity to hold a grudge. These men knew better than anyone Virgil's unforgiving nature.

Kara slowly blew out a strained breath when she approached the men. Six pairs of eyes were now staring intently at her. "Hello, guys. Good seeing you again," she said, fighting back her nervousness.

Not surprisingly, it was Uriel who responded. He was the oldest of the six and she figured he'd decided to take the initiative to be the spokesman. "Kara. It's good seeing you, as well."

"Thanks. And I understand congratulations are in order, Uriel, Winston, Xavier and York, on your marriages." Earlier she had noticed the women they were with. All beautiful women.

The four men said thanks simultaneously.

She then turned her attention to Zion. "And I want to congratulate you, as well, Zion. Your jewelry is beautiful and your success is much deserved." Zion, the youngest of the six, was a world-renowned jewelry

14

maker who'd received international acclaim after being selected as the First Lady's personal jeweler.

"Thanks, Kara."

Everyone had responded to her in some way except Virgil. He just stood there and continued to stare at her. His eyes were so cold she felt the icy chill all the way to her bones. She took a deep breath and then said, "Hello, Virgil."

He didn't return her greeting, just continued to give her a cold stare. But she pushed on. "May I speak with you privately for a minute?"

"No. We have nothing to say to each other."

Virgil's tone was so hard Kara was tempted to turn and walk away. But she refused to do that. She would get him alone even if she had to provoke him into it. She lifted her chin, met his gaze and smiled ruefully. "I understand your not wanting to risk being alone with me, Virgil. Especially since you've never been able to control yourself where I'm concerned."

The narrowing of Virgil's eyes indicated she might have gone too far by bringing up their past relationship and reminding him of how taken he'd once been with her.

He continued to stare at her for the

longest time. Silence surrounded the group and she figured Virgil was well aware the two of them had not only drawn the attention of his godbrothers but a few others in the room who'd known they'd once been a hot item.

Finally Virgil slowly nodded. "You want to talk privately, Kara?" he asked in a clipped voice that was shrouded with a daring tone, one that warned she might regret the request. "Then by all means, lead the way."

Virgil followed Kara as she made her way through the crowded ballroom. He thought she was headed toward the patio, but instead she turned and opened the door that connected to a hallway where several small meeting rooms were located. Evidently she wasn't going to risk their conversation being overheard.

Honestly, he didn't give a royal damn. She was lucky he hadn't called her out right in the middle of the ballroom and told her just what he thought of the comment she'd made. The only thing that had held him in check was the warning looks he'd gotten from his godbrothers to behave himself. He reminded himself that Kara Goshay meant nothing to him anymore. No matter what she thought, she was the last woman who could tempt his control while he was alone with her.

"I don't plan on going any farther, so say whatever you have to say right here, Kara."

She stopped walking, turned around and met his gaze. He thought the same thing tonight he'd thought the first time he'd met her almost five years ago. Kara had the most striking eyes of any woman he'd ever seen. They were a silvery gray and were perfect for her almond-colored complexion. That hadn't been her only asset to grab his attention the night they'd met. She was a bona fide female from top to bottom. Even now he couldn't keep his gaze from trailing from the soles of her stilettos, up her shapely legs, past a small waist and perfect breasts before pausing briefly to take in the mass of medium brown curls around her shoulders. Topping everything off was a very beautiful face.

And then there was the gown she was wearing. The peach mermaid style made her resemble a goddess. He couldn't help noticing when she'd been walking ahead of him how it hugged every curve and flared around her legs at the bottom, giving her a graceful yet sensual appeal. It was as if the gown had been made just for her.

He drew in an angry breath. How was it

possible that after all she'd done to him . . . to them . . . he could still find her extremely attractive and so desirable? At the moment, he refused to acknowledge that even with all the animosity he felt toward her, the air around them crackled with sexual tension and awareness.

Narrowing his gaze, he said, "You've got one minute."

He watched as she breathed in deeply, which made her breasts appear to press even more against the evening gown she was wearing. How he'd loved her breasts — He cut off the memory, frowning as he wondered why he was thinking about that now.

"All right," she said softly, breaking into his thoughts. "I wanted to speak with you privately, Virgil, to apologize. I found out a few days ago that Marti lied to me about you."

If she thought her apology exonerated her for not trusting him, then she was wrong. "It took you four years to find out just what a liar your sister is? Honestly, I could care less what you now know, Kara."

"Will you accept my apology?"

"No."

"No?" She actually sounded surprised.

"No. Why should I? I tried to convince you of my innocence and you refused to believe me. Instead you chose to believe your sister's lies. So now you've found out the truth and expect me to forgive you for throwing away all we had? No."

"I had no idea Marti would deliberately lie about you."

"You should have trusted me enough to believe I would not have betrayed you. Without trust, love is nothing and you proved what we shared was nothing."

He then glanced at his watch. "Now if you will excuse me, your minute is up."

Without giving her a chance to say anything else, he turned and headed down the hallway that led back to the ballroom.

CHAPTER 1

Six months later

"How was the wedding?"

Virgil glanced up when his father walked into his office. For a minute he had forgotten his old man had arrived in town that morning. While growing up Matthew Bougard had been his idol and he still was. Although it seemed that lately, as they both got older, father and son didn't always agree on things. He couldn't help wondering what had brought his father back to Charlotte that morning. All the text message he'd received last night had said was to expect him around ten. And like clockwork, he was here.

"The wedding was nice, although it's hard to believe another Steele got married. Tyson surprised all of us."

Matthew chuckled as he took the chair across from Virgil's desk. "I can imagine. But did you honestly think those Steeles

21

would be die-hard bachelors forever? Take a look at your own godbrothers." The Steele family were good friends of theirs.

Virgil frowned. "I'd rather not." Doing so would make him recall how he and his five godbrothers had formed the Guarded Hearts Club almost four years ago, right after his breakup with Kara Goshay. At the time all six godbrothers had been going through their own personal hell with women and made a pledge to remain single forever. Now four had defected. He and Zion were the only unmarried members left and they were determined to keep the club going, no matter what.

"Well, I am proud of my four godsons and their decisions to settle down and marry. Look at your mom and me, Virgil. We've been happily married close to forty years now."

Virgil hoped his father wasn't about to start his never-ending sermon about love, happiness and the pursuit of marriage. He'd heard it enough over the years; hearing it again wouldn't change a thing. Yes, he knew his parents had a long and happy marriage. He knew his father considered his mother his queen and she considered Matthew her king. He even knew — although he'd rather not think about it — that they still had a very active sex life. He'd discovered that upon arriving in the Keys unexpectedly last summer to join them on their vacation. It was supposed to be a surprise for them but ended up being a shocker for him when he'd walked in on his parents making out like teens.

Matthew and Rhona had met while attending college in Atlanta. His father had graduated from Morehouse and his mother from Clark Atlanta University. Instead of returning to Houston, where he'd been born and raised, Matthew asked Rhona to marry him and they settled in her hometown of Charlotte, North Carolina.

Just in case a sermon was on his father's agenda, Virgil quickly asked, "So, Dad, what brings you back to Charlotte?"

His father was still CEO of Bougard Enterprises, though he rarely came into the office anymore, leaving Virgil, as second in command, to make most of the day-to-day decisions. His parents were often busy traveling, and just last year they'd bought a home in Houston with the intention of spending more time there.

But Matthew Bougard was well aware of every aspect of BE's business. He was sharp and highly intelligent, which was how he'd taken a small financial company he'd founded right out of college and made it into one of the largest hedge fund corporations in the country. And thanks to a few recent deals, they could now even boast of going global.

His father remained quiet for a moment and then said, "I'm thinking about retiring, Virgil."

Virgil sat up straight in his chair. "You really mean it this time?"

Matthew chuckled. "Yes. Leigh informed us on Friday that she and Chad are expecting a baby," his father said, beaming heartily. "That means your mom and I will be grandparents."

Virgil couldn't help but smile. He knew how much being grandparents meant to them. His younger sister had married her childhood sweetheart a few years ago after they both finished medical school. Last year Leigh and Chad had opened a medical complex in Houston and were doing just great.

"I need to call Leigh and Chad to congratulate them. Congratulations to you and Mom, as well," Virgil said.

"Thanks. I'd like to spend more time in the Keys as well as in Houston. Plus I promised your mom we'd do more international travel. She really enjoyed that Mediterranean cruise I took her on last year."

His father leaned back in his chair and studied him. From the close scrutiny, Virgil got the feeling there was more to come regarding his father's pending retirement. "My decision to retire depends on you, Virgil."

Virgil lifted a brow. "How does your decision to retire depend on me?"

His father leaned forward and Virgil knew this would be one of those Matthew Bougard deeply serious moments. Virgil wasn't sure if he was mentally prepared for it this early in the morning.

"You have a reputation, Virgil."

He didn't have to wonder what his father was alluding to. It was well-known around Charlotte and the surrounding areas that Virgil Matthew Bougard was an ardent womanizer. As far as he was concerned, he had no reason not to be if that was the lifestyle he chose. He wasn't married, nor was he in an exclusive relationship with any woman. So in his defense he could do whatever the hell he wanted to do and with whomever he chose.

"I'm a thirty-five-year-old single man, Dad. There's no reason I shouldn't enjoy female company whenever I want it."

"Well, there's that incident with Whitney

Hilton that won't go away as much as I wish it would. Marv Hilton hasn't forgotten about it."

Virgil released a deep sigh. That had been almost two years ago. Why couldn't the man get over it? Would that be the scandal that haunted him forever? Marv Hilton had been one of their biggest clients and Whitney was his twenty-five-year-old daughter. Her father had brought her along on one of his business trips to Hawaii when BE had held a meeting at the same time.

"She came to my hotel room. I didn't go to hers."

"I know but to Marv none of that matters. You slept with his daughter, and as her father, he was livid."

Virgil recalled the man had been so livid that he'd dropped his account with Bougard Enterprises. Drawing in a deep breath, he could now admit when he'd gotten out of the shower and found Whitney naked and stretched out on his bed, he should have tossed her out of his room. But that option had quickly left his mind when she'd proceeded to give him one badass blow job. Her father had found out about the incident, which Virgil suspected had been intentional. Whitney wanted to get back at her father for forcing her into an engagement with some rich, old oil baron from Texas.

"That was almost two years ago, Dad."

"Yes, but Marv Hilton still wants blood, especially since her fiancé called off the wedding. Marv blames you for that. He swears his daughter was a virgin up to that time and she was saving herself for her wedding. However, I'm sure you know better."

Yes, Virgil definitely knew better since Whitney had boasted about her very active sex life that night. And the only thing she was saving was herself — from being forced into marrying a man old enough to be her father.

"You've done a great job running things in my absence, Virgil." His father intruded into his thoughts. "And there's no doubt in my mind the company would be in good hands if I were to retire. But we have to do something about cleaning up your image, especially if we want Paul Wyman's business. He and I have talked. But he's heard about you from Hilton, and Wyman has three daughters he's concerned about."

Virgil's gaze narrowed. "You make me sound like someone who goes after anything in a skirt."

"Well, that's the impression that's out there and Hilton is milking it for all it's worth. Such an image could eventually hurt the company."

Virgil stood, walked over to the window and stared out at downtown Charlotte. It was the second week in August and already the sun was beating down, guaranteeing it would be another hot day. Drawing in a deep breath, he slowly turned around.

Knowing his father, Virgil was certain the old man had a plan, one he'd thought out thoroughly. That's the way Matthew Bougard worked. If there was a problem, he came up with a solution. Virgil just hoped it was one he could go along with. "Okay, what do you suggest?"

"I think we should hire a good PR consultant, one who will come in and clean up your womanizing image."

Virgil frowned. "Do you really think that's necessary, Dad?"

"Yes. Hilton is claiming that you seduced his daughter. So I hope you can see the need to take proactive measures."

Virgil walked back over to his desk and sat down. Like his father said, Marv Hilton was out for blood. His. Unfortunately the man ran in circles with people who were potential clients for Bougard Enterprises.

"Fine. Do what you think is best. If you

think hiring a PR firm will work, let's do it."

"I figured you would understand, so for the past couple of weeks I've been checking out firms. The one I suggest using comes highly recommended."

"Great," he said drily. "What's the name of the company?"

"Goshay PR and Image Consultants."

Virgil was out of his seat in a flash. "That's out of the question. You know Kara owns that business."

"Yes."

Virgil was fuming. "Then why on earth would you want to hire her?"

"Calm down, Virgil. The reason I'm hiring Kara's company is because she's the best. Anyone who could clean up Senator Jack Payne's reputation after that scandal involving him and those women — and get him reelected — can surely clean up yours without a problem."

Matthew stared hard at him, and continued, "Why are you so upset about it? Are you admitting you've only been lying to yourself these past four years and that you do still care for Kara?"

"No! I care nothing for her." It had taken a long time for him to finally reach that point, but he had. At one time he'd thought it would be nearly impossible to ever get her out of his heart.

"Then working with her shouldn't be a problem for you."

"It will be a problem because I prefer not being anywhere near her."

"Then maybe you need to ask yourself why."

Virgil shook his head. "You don't understand, Dad."

"What I understand is, because of her lack of trust in you, you won't forgive her and you're still holding a grudge. But then so is Marv Hilton. That's why Kara's services are needed."

Virgil didn't say anything but walked back to the window to stare out. A few moments later he turned to his father. "I prefer we go with some other company, Dad."

"Unless you can give me a good reason why Kara can't do the job, Virgil, she's in."

Virgil drew in a deep breath. There was no need to tell his dad that Kara had been the only woman he had ever loved. Both his parents knew that. But they didn't know he had planned to propose to her the same week she had hurled her accusations against him.

"Level with me, Virgil. The last thing I need to worry about is you trying to seduce

Kara. She's getting hired to do a job. So if you think you still feel anything for her then —"

"Oh, I feel something for her all right," Virgil said in an angry tone. "I feel so much dislike for her you can whip it into butter. So I honestly don't see how I'll be able to work with her."

"For Bougard Enterprises it's business, Virgil. For you, it sounds like a personal problem you need to work through. The way I see it, you could have sent Whitney Hilton from your room that night but you didn't. Instead you chose to let her stay. It was your decision and with that decision came consequences this company has to deal with. I would love to retire and spend more time with your mother and my future grandchild, but I'll hang around if I have to."

Virgil definitely didn't want that. As much as he loved his father and appreciated his wisdom and expertise, Virgil had gotten used to making the decisions. He was ready to handle things without the old man. If his father thought he needed an image adjustment, then fine. "You win, Dad. Go ahead and hire Kara's company."

Matthew stood. "It's not about winning, Virgil. It's about making the right moves to ensure that Bougard Enterprises will be around for a long time. I'll have my administrative assistant call Kara to come in so we can discuss our plan with her."

Virgil drew in a deep breath. He would have to put up with Kara . . . or die trying.

Kara hung up the phone with a shocked look on her face. Of all things . . . A call from Matthew Bougard's administrative assistant saying he wanted to meet with her tomorrow to discuss a possible job offer.

She leaned back in her chair. Just what did Bougard Enterprises need? Considering her strained relationship with Virgil, which she figured Mr. Bougard had to know about, she was surprised he'd reached out to her company, despite its excellent reputation. She'd find out soon enough what Matthew Bougard wanted.

Will Virgil be at the meeting?

Tossing a paper clip on her desk, Kara thrust the question from her mind. Sure, he'd be there. And it was no big deal, she told herself. She recalled her last meeting with Virgil six months ago when she had apologized. She would always regret believing Marti's lie and what doing so had cost her. She had not spoken to her sister since finding out the truth. As far as Kara was concerned, they didn't have anything to say to each other. She loved Marti but Kara could never forget the day she'd arrived back in town early from a business trip. She'd gone to her sister's office to invite her to lunch only to overhear Marti telling someone on the phone how she had lied to Kara. Marti had claimed she had seen Virgil having a romantic dinner with a woman and had followed them all the way to a hotel and watched them go inside.

When Kara had confronted her, she had admitted lying and said she had done it for Kara's own good, as it would have been just a matter of time before Virgil hurt her. To Kara, that excuse was unacceptable.

The buzzing on her desk brought her thoughts back to the present. "Yes, Janice?"

"Your mother is on line one."

Kara drew in a deep breath. Her mother was the last person she wanted to talk to. To Lydia Goshay's way of thinking it was past time Kara forgave her sister.

"Tell my mother I'm in a meeting and I'll call her back later."

At the moment, Kara didn't want to talk to anyone. All she wanted to do was to relax her mind for a minute. That call from Bougard Enterprises had definitely rattled her brain. Leaning back in her chair she closed her eyes and, it seemed of its own accord, her mind began reliving memories of that night five years ago when she and Virgil had met.

"May I have this dance?"

Kara's heart began pounding the minute she turned to stare up into what had to be the most gorgeous pair of brown eyes she'd ever seen. Bedroom eyes. They were an indulgent chocolate hue that made one think of something totally sweet and clandestinely sinful.

Although they had never been formally introduced, she knew who he was. Virgil Bougard. He had a reputation around town that would make Casanova look like a choir boy. His name was often whispered on women's lips followed by a salacious smile. She'd first heard about him in the locker room at her gym. Women claimed he was hot, both in and out of bed. They also claimed he was a man who got any woman he wanted. And she had a feeling that tonight for some reason she had caught his eye.

She'd seen him when he'd arrived and had watched how several women had put themselves in his path. It seemed he drew them to him like a magnet. But he hadn't danced with anyone. His attention had seemed targeted on her.

For most of the night their gazes had been

meeting and holding from across the room. Each time she could feel her blood rush through her veins. She had noticed how impeccably he was dressed and how tall he stood, an imposing figure against any other man in the room. Talk about sex appeal.

She wished she could say it was all due to his ultra-handsome looks, consisting of an angular face that boasted a firm jaw, full lips and high cheekbones. And when he'd smiled her stomach did a couple of flips, and then she saw the dimples in those cheeks.

And now that same man was standing right in front of her, asking her to dance. Although she wished otherwise, she could feel heat swirling through her. She felt an intense sexual connection between them and couldn't understand how that could be. Although she knew better and was totally aware of his scandalous reputation around town, she was shamefully attracted to him.

"Dance?" she repeated.

The way his mouth curved in a teasing smile made more curling heat settle in the pit of her stomach. "Yes, dance. I would do just about anything to hold you in my arms."

Kara couldn't believe this stranger would be so audacious as to say that.

"Who are you?" she asked. She knew his identity but felt he should introduce himself nonetheless.

He gave her another smile. "Virgil. Virgil Bougard. And you're . . . ?"

"Kara Goshay."

"Nice meeting you, Kara." He paused a moment and then asked, "So . . . are we going to dance?"

She didn't miss the desire smoldering in the depths of those bedroom eyes. The sight of it made her heart rate accelerate in her chest. "Yes, Virgil. I will dance with you."

Kara slowly opened her eyes and drew in a deep breath. They had danced. More than once.

Believing Marti's lie was something she would regret for the rest of her life. Because in doing so, she had lost the one man she would ever love.

CHAPTER 2

Virgil entered his home and tossed his jacket across a chair. At least his father's visit hadn't stopped him from sticking with his plan to leave work early. He needed to rest, relax and recover from too much partying this weekend at Tyson's wedding. Now he had another reason for needing down time. Namely to get his mind prepared for tomorrow's meeting with Kara.

She had done something no one had thought was possible, which was to literally bring him to his knees and show him there was a difference between love and lust. His womanizing ways had begun to morph into those of a man who wanted only one woman. Her. She had singlehandedly transformed his reckless heart into a thoughtful one.

That was then. This was now.

He was no longer a fool in love. And Kara was someone he could do without. He staunchly refused to give his heart to another woman, and he enjoyed his time as a single man who wore no female's heart on his sleeve. He was a card-carrying member of the Guarded Hearts Club.

Over the years the club had seen its membership dwindle. Uriel had dropped out when he married Ellie. A year later Xavier had married Farrah, followed by York marrying Darcy and then Winston tying the knot with Ainsley. The last one had been a shocker because no one had been a stronger advocate of bachelorhood than Winston. Hell, Winston even held the office of club president for a number of years. That left only him and Zion as lone members. As the president, he felt it was time they recruited new members.

Although the club started out exclusively for him and his godbrothers, that didn't mean it had to stay that way. There had to be other single men who felt the same way they did. Men who enjoyed the single life and intended to never marry. Mercury and Gannon Steele headed the list. It wouldn't be hard to convince them that bachelors needed to stick together and they needed to join the exclusive club. He'd heard the frustration in their voices this weekend at Tyson's wedding. Mercury and Gannon figured it would only be a matter of time before their mother eyed one of them as the next possible groom.

And then there was Xavier's friend Kurt. He would be another good candidate. And wasn't it just last week that Quade Westmoreland, who was an in-law of those Steeles, mention something about newfound bachelor cousins living somewhere in Alaska? A semblance of a smile touched Virgil's face. There was hope after all.

A frown replaced the smile when his thoughts shifted to Whitney Hilton. She had definitely been a mistake and one he was still paying for. It wasn't as if Whitney had been an underage teenager. Hell, the woman had been twenty-five. An adult. A consenting adult. Hilton was disillusioned if he thought his daughter had been a virgin that night. Nevertheless, for one night of lust, he would pay by having to put up with Kara. That was something he didn't look forward to doing.

As he headed for the kitchen to grab a cold beer out of the refrigerator, he couldn't help allowing his mind to recall a time when Kara's presence was the only thing he'd wanted.

And it had started with their first dance . . .

■ ■ ■ ■

"So, Kara, tell me about yourself."

Virgil couldn't help looking into her eyes when he'd made the request. She was simply beautiful. Striking. Stunning. And the dress she was wearing showed off her body right down to every curve. He wanted to get to know her but there were other things he wanted to do to her, as well. Taste her. Touch her. But for now, dancing with her had to suffice.

He had noticed her the moment he'd entered the ballroom and had known then she was someone he had to connect with. Each time their gazes had linked, he'd felt stirring emotions he had never felt before. There was no way he could have not sought her out. They had introduced themselves and now he wanted to know everything there was to know about her. Then maybe he could figure out why she was having such an effect on him. No woman had ever rattled his senses like she was doing.

"There's not a whole lot to tell," she said. "I was born in San Francisco twenty-five years ago. My parents are still there, both alive and well, and I have a sister, who is older than me by three years. I got my degree in marketing from Duke and landed a job here in Charlotte right after college. Last year I opened my own PR firm."

She felt good in his arms and he liked the way his arms fit around her waist. "Are you dating?"

"Sometimes."

"Seeing anyone exclusively?"

"No."

"Good."

She raised a brow and he could only smile. And before she could ask he said, "The reason I think it's good is because I want you for myself."

She tilted her head to study him and even raised her chin showing a little irritation at his audacity. His intent was unmistakable. His smile deepened, clearly unmoved that what he'd said might have possibly annoyed her. He believed in being honest with women. Game playing wasn't his style. "And what if I'm not interested, Virgil?"

"Then it would be my job to get you interested. But I think we can toss out that possibility. You're just as interested in me as I am in you."

He could tell her irritation increased. "What makes you think so?"

He shrugged. "A number of things, including body language. But primarily the way we've been flirting with each other most of night."

"Is that what you think? That I've been flirting with you from across the room?"

"Haven't you? But then I'll admit unashamedly that I've been flirting with you, as well. Now I think we should move beyond flirting."

"Do you?"

"Yes." He held her gaze while she stared at him. The sway of their bodies in tune with the music was a no-thought process, and it was a good thing since they were so focused on each other. He especially liked the feel of their bodies touching while they danced.

"And just where are we supposed to be moving to?" she asked. For her to have done so meant she was giving the idea some thought.

"I'm hoping I can entice you to leave here with me and . . ."

When he felt her tense, he said smoothly, "Go to an all-night café not far from here and share a cup of coffee with me. That way we can get to know each other even better."

She relaxed and he was grateful for that. The last thing he wanted to do was give her the impression all he wanted was to take her to the nearest hotel or back to her place or his. Doing any of the three would definitely work for him since he wanted her just that much. However, he had a feeling she was not a one-night-stand kind of woman, even though he had no problem being a one-night-stand kind of man when it suited him. He had a feeling he would have to work his way into her bed. He didn't mind that and figured she would be worth it in the end.

"I'll think about it . . . the part about the all-night café. But you haven't told me anything about yourself."

A smile touched his lips. He had no problem doing that. "I'm thirty and the oldest of two. I have a sister who is four years younger. She's single but dates her high school sweetheart. I figure they'll get married one of these days. I work at Bougard Enterprises, a financial corporation founded by my father years ago. He's brilliant when it comes to finance and I'm learning all that I can from him. He's been hinting at retiring in a few years."

"And when he does, that means more work for you, right?"

"Yes, but I love what I do. I guess it's in my blood."

Much too soon the music came to an end. Without questioning why such a thing mattered to him, he kept a firm grip on her arm. Instead of leading her back to where she'd been standing before the dance, he led her toward the patio. "It's a beautiful night. Let's appreciate it, all right?"

"Okay."

He couldn't help but smile as he led her through the huge French doors and outside. For some reason he felt tonight would be his lucky night.

Virgil took a huge swig of his beer, bringing his thoughts back to the present. Had it been his lucky night? It depended on how he looked at it. Yes, they'd left the party early to share cups of coffee at that café, and, yes, from that night and for a full year after that, they'd dated exclusively. He chuckled, thinking she hadn't been as easy as he thought to get into bed. She had made him earn that right and he'd felt it had been worth it. She had been worth it. And he had fallen hopelessly in love. Their time together had been happy times . . . till they were tinged with heartache when she'd accused him of being involved with another woman.

When he saw her tomorrow he would be as professional as he could, no matter how much he would hate every minute of doing so. He didn't want to give anyone, especially his father, the impression that he felt anything for her anymore.

He finished off the rest of his beer and was about to change into more comfortable clothing when his mobile phone went off.

He recognized the ringtone. Each of his godbrothers had their own specific ring. "What's up, W? Calling all the way from Australia is probably costing you a pretty penny, isn't it?"

Over the years he and his godbrothers had shortened their names for each other to just the first letter. Winston, a marine biologist, and his wife, Ainsley, were currently living in Australia near the Great Barrier Reef on some project dealing with sea turtles.

"Just giving all of you a heads-up that I'll be home next month."

Virgil chuckled. "You were home six months ago. Getting homesick?"

Winston returned his chuckle. "No. Ainsley and I love it here. Six months ago we were home for her parents' wedding anniversary. This time it's for Uriel. Have you forgotten his birthday is next month? I talked to Ellie and she's throwing a party at the lake and would like all of us there." He paused a moment and then asked, "How are things going with you, V?"

He knew why Winston was asking. When he was home back in February, Virgil and his godbrothers had been together at the charity ball when Virgil had seen Kara. They knew what Kara had once meant to him and were glad she'd finally found out the truth about her sister. They'd also thought it had taken a lot of guts for her to apologize, considering how he'd been staring her down all night. And last but not least, they all thought he should have accepted the apology she offered. They felt he should be able to forgive Kara even if he didn't want to have anything to do with her ever again.

Virgil didn't see it that way. He saw no reason to release her from the guilt of accusing him of something he hadn't done. "Things are okay," he finally said. "Tyson's wedding went off without a hitch. In fact, he had that same lovesick look that you did at your wedding."

"It's the 'I'm in love' look, Virgil. I recall you once wore it yourself."

"That was when I didn't know any better. It was before I talked you guys into forming the club. The one you, York, Xavier and Uriel defected from."

"Only to pursue happier days."

"If you say so," Virgil said, shaking his head.

"Have you seen Kara since that night, V?"

Virgil frowned. "Why would I see her after that night?"

"Um, maybe you've had a change of heart. Called her. Asked her out for old times' sake."

"Don't hold your breath. But I will be seeing her tomorrow. Not my choice, believe me."

"Why? What's going on?"

He then told Winston about his father's plan to improve his image.

"Well, I hope you don't plan to be an obnoxious ass when you see her. She did apologize. And can you imagine having a sister like Marti?"

Most of his godbrothers knew Marti because she'd dated Xavier. According to Xavier, three weeks was all he could take of Marti Goshay, who thought a lot of herself. Even Virgil would admit it was hard to believe Marti and Kara were siblings. They were as different as night and day.

"Can you imagine how Kara must feel knowing her sister lied? If you can't trust your sibling, then who can you trust?"

Virgil decided not to answer that. In fact he really didn't want to discuss the Goshay sisters any longer. He deliberately got Winston to talk about something else — namely his work. Winston loved what he did for a living and went on to tell Virgil how his research on the turtles was coming.

When Winston began getting too scientific, Virgil decided it was time to end their conversation. "We'll get together when you arrive in town, W."

"You bet. Take care."

"You, too."

"And remember to be nice tomorrow, V."

"I'll try. Can't make any promises."

Virgil clicked off the phone. Dread filled him as he thought about tomorrow. Just like he told Winston, as far as being nice to Kara went, all he could do was try.

CHAPTER 3

Kara paused to draw in a deep breath, needing to calm her frayed nerves. She was ten minutes early so why were the Bougards already in the conference room waiting on her? And the thought that one of them had seen her naked probably just as many times as he'd seen her wearing clothes was enough to rattle her.

Shaking off the memories of all those times, she thought about one of her favorite quotes. *You are stronger than you think.* She certainly hoped so because at the moment she felt a little weak in the knees. And what were those sensuous shivers racing through her? Now was not the time to remember any of that. Straightening her spine, raising her chin and pasting a professional smile on her lips, she turned the knob and entered the conference room.

Both men stood and, although she hadn't wanted it to, her gaze immediately went to

Virgil before shifting to the older Bougard. She liked Virgil's father and could easily recall when Virgil had taken her home to meet his parents. She'd been nervous then, as well.

Like Virgil, Matthew Bougard was handsome. He was also tall, standing way over six feet, and had a muscular build. She knew he liked playing golf and he'd been on the Olympic swim team while in college at Morehouse.

"I hope I haven't kept you waiting," she said, and with all the professionalism she could muster, she crossed the room and extended her hand first to Matthew. Instead of taking it, he pulled her to him in a hug. "No, you're early, in fact. We just didn't want to keep you waiting on us. It's good seeing you again, Kara."

When he released her, she smiled up at him. "Good seeing you again, too, Matthew. How's Rhona?"

"She's fine and sends her love."

Kara then shifted her gaze to Virgil. He was standing beside his father, impeccably dressed in a dark business suit. She wished she wasn't so intensely aware of him and wished more than anything that seeing him didn't remind her of how long she'd been without a man. After him and the pain she'd felt at the time, she had sworn off men.

His expression was unreadable when he said, "Kara, glad you could meet with us today." He extended his hand to her, letting her know that if she assumed he would pull her into his arms for a hug like his father had, then she was wrong.

Kara took the hand Virgil offered and tried not to show any sort of reaction when a frisson of heat raced up her spine. "Glad I'm meeting with the two of you, as well."

Although he didn't say anything, something in his eyes told her that her presence here today hadn't been his idea. She pulled her hand from Virgil's and then said to both men, "I'm eager to find out why you feel that you need my services."

"And we're eager to tell you so you can get started on our problem right away," Matthew said, smiling. "Please have a seat."

"Thanks." She sat down in the chair Matthew had pulled out for her, the one right across from Virgil.

She tried to ignore his intense stare or at least try to. "So what's the problem?" she asked, darting her gaze between the two men.

It was Virgil who spoke. "It seems my image needs improving."

She raised an eyebrow. "Your image?"

It was Matthew who then added, rather bluntly, "Yes, his image. Everyone thinks my son's behavior is that of a manwhore, and it's hurting business. We want to hire your company to improve his image."

Virgil frowned at his father. "Manwhore? I wouldn't go that far, Dad."

"I didn't say you were one, Virgil. I said that's the perception out there and it's hurting the company."

Virgil wished he could say "damn the company," but he loved Bougard Enterprises just as much as his dad did. He would do anything to make sure the company his father had started years ago did not fail under his watch. Even if it meant making sacrifices. Still, he couldn't help saying, "I enjoy women and like I told you yesterday, Dad, as a single man there's nothing wrong with my dating habits."

Okay, he would admit he dated a lot of women, but being thought of as a manwhore was a bit too much. The only good thing about his father's statement was that it was painting a picture for Kara that he'd successfully moved on and put her behind him.

But even with all the pain she'd caused him, he could say without a doubt that Kara

Goshay was the most beautiful woman he'd ever met. Not too many could go from being a staunch businesswoman to a slinky seductress in the blink of an eye.

It had taken every ounce of strength he had to control himself when she'd walked into the room with that sensuous and graceful movement of hers. Six months ago when he'd seen her at that charity event, she'd been wearing an eye-catching evening gown. Today she was dressed in a tan business suit with matching pumps. He'd always thought he was a stilettos man but he had to admit her legs looked gorgeous in a pair of pumps.

Why was he thinking about that? And why was his mind filled with the memory of taking a business suit — similar to the one she was wearing — off her one night? Piece by piece. Bit by bit. And why was he remembering how good she looked naked, how smooth her skin was and how soft she was to his touch?

Her hair hung in soft layers around her shoulders and the little makeup she wore did what it was supposed to do, which was to enhance her looks and not cover them. And were those pearl earrings in her ears the same ones he'd given her when they had celebrated their first Christmas together? If so, why was she wearing them today? Did she think doing so would move him in some way? Make him remember the good times? Forget about the bad? If she thought that, then she was wrong. He was so over her.

"As far as something being wrong with your dating habits, our major investors apparently think so," Matthew said, breaking into Virgil's thoughts. "So what about it, Kara? Can he be helped?"

Kara didn't say anything for a moment. Matthew's words about Virgil's wretched reputation hadn't been a shock. Since their breakup she'd heard he had gone back to his womanizing ways.

Matthew and Virgil were waiting for her response . . . at least she figured Matthew was. Virgil sat there wearing one of those "I don't give a damn what anyone thinks" expressions. That made her wonder if he was willing to change his lifestyle for the sake of his company, which prompted her ultimate response. "I can only help if Virgil wants to be helped."

Virgil decided to speak up. It was time he let both Kara and his father know that this change in his image had limitations. "I'm a single man who's not in an exclusive relationship with any woman. I enjoy dating and if anyone has an issue with that then that's their problem and not mine."

Matthew turned to him. "But you would agree after the Whitney Hilton scandal that your image needs an overhaul?"

Not really, he thought. Whitney had gotten just what she'd come to his hotel room for that night. She'd been happy. He'd been satisfied. It was her father who refused to accept that his daughter had an active sex life — before, during and after Virgil Bougard.

"Is that something I need to know about? The scandal with Whitney Hilton?" Kara asked.

As far as Virgil was concerned it wasn't any of her business. But evidently his father didn't see it that way.

"Whitney Hilton is the daughter of one of my biggest clients," Matthew said. "At least I should say former clients. During a business trip almost two years ago, Whitney tagged along with her father. She took a liking to Virgil and ended up in his hotel room one night. It caused a little ruckus when her fiancé found out and broke their engagement. Her father was livid and accused Virgil of deflowering his daughter. Claimed she was saving herself for her husband. Since then Marv Hilton has tried to tarnish our company's good name with potential clients."

Kara looked over at Virgil, cocked her head. "Do you know if she was a virgin as her father claims?"

Virgil frowned. "No. That's the lie Marv Hilton wants to believe. But then that's the thing about lies. They are meant to be believed, especially by those who're gullible enough to do so."

Kara didn't have to wonder if what he'd said was meant to be a dig because she knew that it had been. "How old was she?"

"At the time Whitney was twenty-five."

"Twenty-five?" Kara asked, surprised. "So she wasn't a child but an adult who was old enough to make her own decisions."

"You tell that to her old man" was Virgil's flippant response. "It's my guess she would have done anything to get out of marrying the man her father had picked out for her. Some oilman from Texas who was old enough to be her father. And she used me to do it. She had a reason for coming to my room and then making sure both her father and fiancé found out about it."

"So what do you think, Kara?" Matthew broke in to her thoughts to ask. "Can his image be fixed?"

Before she could sufficiently answer that, she needed to make sure Virgil was 100 percent on board with an image makeover.

If he wasn't then he would only be wasting her time and his company's money. "Not sure," she answered Matthew while holding Virgil's gaze. "Virgil still hasn't answered the question I put out there a while ago."

She watched Virgil's lips twitch in annoyance. "What question?"

"The one I posed as to whether or not you want to be helped. I need to know if you will allow me to do my job to improve your image."

The room had gotten quiet, and he knew that his dad, as well as Kara, was waiting on his response. "Fine, knock yourself out."

"In other words you will do it and not give Kara a hard time doing so, right?" His father turned and asked him with those razor sharp eyes that all but said to leave the bullshit at the door.

"Yes, Dad. Right now my main concern is keeping Bougard Enterprises at the top."

"Good." As if what Virgil had said was enough to satisfy him, Matthew Bougard stood and looked at his watch. "The two of you can work out all the finer details of what needs to be done. As for me, I've kept my queen waiting long enough. Rhona and I are joining friends for lunch at the Racetrack Café."

The café, which was jointly owned by

several drivers on the NASCAR circuit, including a friend of his by the name of Bronson Scott, had the best hamburgers and fries in Charlotte. "I hope you and Mom enjoy lunch with your friends, Dad."

"And we will, especially since I know this matter of your image will be resolved with Kara's help." Matthew then turned to Kara. "I appreciate your handling this for us."

He paused a minute and then said, "I'm going to tell you just what I told Virgil yesterday. No matter how the two of you feel about each other, this here is business. The reason you're being hired is because I believe you are the best person to do what needs to be done, Kara. I expect you and Virgil to put aside whatever differences you have and act like professionals. And I'm sure the two of you will."

With that said, Matthew Bougard opened the conference room door and walked out, leaving Kara and Virgil staring uneasily at each other.

CHAPTER 4

"Well, he certainly said a mouthful," Virgil said moments later, breaking the silence in the room.

"And I can understand his concern." Kara pushed back her chair and stood. "But I'm sure you and I will handle ourselves as the professionals that we are. What happened to end our relationship was unfortunate. It was a mistake on my part. I apologized. You didn't accept my apology. There's nothing I can do about that but move on and not worry about it. And I have."

She saw Virgil's body tighten as he gazed up at her. "Did you really expect me to accept your apology?"

She shrugged. "Don't know why you wouldn't. It was made in all sincerity. I admitted I was wrong. My conscience is clear."

He frowned as he stood, as well. "Your conscience is clear? I don't see how it can be," he said in a gruff voice.

Kara couldn't help but study the features of the man standing before her. He was handsome to the point where the word *eye candy* just wouldn't do him justice. But as she stared into his brown eyes, she saw something that made her swallow hard. His inability to forgive. It was there in the dark depths of the eyes gazing back at her, letting her know he was barely tolerating her presence.

"Well, let me tell you how that can be, Virgil," Kara said, staring him down. Frankly, she was sick and tired of his attitude. He acted as if he was the only one who'd suffered from Marti's lie.

"I am human. I make mistakes. Big and small. We all do. We also trust and believe in people that we should not. I did. I took Marti's word over yours. Something I will regret doing for the rest of my life. I loved you and —"

"No," Virgil said angrily. "There's no way in hell you can convince me that you loved me. No woman could love a man one minute and then assume the worse of him the next. You only thought you loved me."

She stared at him, knowing it would be a waste of her time to try to convince him otherwise. In his eyes, a woman who loved a man would not have believed the worst of him. But regardless of what he thought, she *had* loved him.

"I apologized to you, Virgil. But you didn't accept it. Great. Fine. That's your prerogative. Mine is to keep moving and keep living. I can't let your inability to forgive hang over my head. There's more to life than living in the past."

She paused a moment and then in a calmer voice said, "I'll start work immediately on a plan of action for your image makeover. I'll call you once it's completed so we can meet to discuss it."

With nothing else to say, she turned and walked out of the office.

Virgil's body stiffened in anger when the door clicked shut behind Kara. She had a lot of nerve. That was all fine and dandy that she could keep moving and keep living; he could make the same claim. But what she failed to take into account was what her belief in her sister's lie had done to him. Had done to them. And he couldn't help noticing she hadn't refuted his words when he said she'd only assumed she loved him. In not doing so, she'd all but admitted he'd been merely an infatuation. That thought angered him even more.

There's more to life than living in the past. Upon remembering Kara's words, it took every ounce of control he had not to go after her and let her know that although he wasn't living in the past, it was the past he'd shared with her that had shaped him into the man he was today. A man determined not to let any woman get close to his heart again. A man who'd been taught there was no such thing as the perfect love. A man who enjoyed being physically involved but emotionally detached from women.

She would never know how she'd nearly destroyed him four years ago. For months he hadn't been able to eat, sleep or function like a sane person. It was only when his god-brothers had talked him into taking one of those singles cruises with them that he'd returned to the land of the living. It had taken him almost a full year to get over Kara, put her behind him. And in doing so, he'd developed an entirely new agenda and game plan when it came to women. He refused to love one, and he lusted for plenty.

And she thought she could wipe the slate clean with just an apology?

Virgil shoved his hands into his pockets as he walked over to the window and looked out. And now they would be working together to improve his image. How crazy was that? He rubbed his hand down his face. *There's more to life than living in the past.*

He forced his mind to rethink Kara's words, this time with deeper meaning and clarity. Maybe by carrying all this bitterness inside of him the way he had, he was living in the past, not letting go of what she had done.

Forgiving didn't mean forgetting. Nor did it mean reconciliation. What they once shared could never be regained. She was totally and completely out of his heart now, so wasn't it time he acted like it? There was no reason why they could not deal with each other on the professional level his father had alluded to. It wasn't about him or her but all about Bougard Enterprises.

Virgil figured one day he would eventually marry, especially since he needed heirs to continue the Bougard legacy. And when he did, it wouldn't be for love. Thanks to Kara Goshay he would know better the next time.

"Your father is on line one, Ms. Goshay."

Kara released a frustrated sigh but couldn't stop the smile that touched her lips. She figured since her mother's attempt to bring an end to her strained relationship with Marti had failed, Lydia had called in the big guns. Namely Byron Goshay. Kara had always been a daddy's girl and proud of it. Her father adored both of his daughters, but there had always been a special bond between the two of them.

"Put him through, please."

Leaning back in her chair, she waited for the connection while recalling her conversation with her mother when she returned her call yesterday. It was a discussion that hadn't gone over well. Lydia tried shifting the blame to Kara, saying she was allowing a man to come between her and her sister. She felt Kara should make up with Marti now that her sister was under a doctor's care for stress and anxiety attacks.

Kara had gotten royally pissed. She sympathized with whatever Marti was going through, but what about those four years Kara had suffered, thinking the man she loved had betrayed her? What about the stress she'd gone through? The heartbreak? The pain? How could one sister do that to another?

"Kara? How's my girl?"

The sound of her father's voice chased away the anger. She smiled. "I'm fine, Dad. What about you?"

"I'm doing okay. Looking forward to retirement in a few years. Just waiting for my daughters to pay off their student loans so they can take care of their old man."

Kara shook her head. "Our student loans are paid off. Besides, you wouldn't accept a handout from me or Marti even if your life depended on it."

She heard her father's chuckle. "True."

He then paused, and she knew what was coming when she detected him shifting to a more serious mode. "Your mom talked to me last night about the ongoing situation between you and Marti."

"And?"

"And I think we need to have a family powwow. A sort of bonding session. I'd like to fly both you and Marti home for the weekend."

As if flying out to San Francisco would magically make things better. "It won't do any good, Dad."

"Sweetheart, Marti's your sister."

So now her father was taking that approach? She couldn't stop the flare of anger. "Yes, and *my sister* deliberately sabotaged my relationship with the man I loved."

There was another pause. "I just want my daughters back together. I feel our family is breaking apart."

"Don't blame me, Dad."

"Of course I don't blame you."

Kara was glad to hear that. "Mom did."

"Lydia should not have said that. I told her we needed to stay out of it and let you and Marti handle things. But I guess she saw that wasn't happening and figured she needed to step in. But that's no reason to blame you. You didn't ask for what Marti did. Have you seen Virgil and told him the truth?"

"Yes, for what good that did. I apologized but he didn't accept my apology. I can't blame him to be honest with you. I said some mean things to him back then. I think now he hates me more than ever."

"Sorry to hear that. I tried calling him to apologize, as well. He's changed his number from the one I had."

Kara lifted a brow. "Why would you need to apologize?"

"Because after the two of you broke up and Marti told me what he did, I called him and said a lot of not-so-nice things to him."

Kara's eyes closed for a minute. Her sister's lie had caused more damage than Kara had realized. "I didn't know," she said softly. Her father had liked Virgil a lot, and vice versa. Getting such a call from her father had probably only added to Virgil's anger. "Why didn't you tell me?"

"At the time I felt there was no reason to tell you. I thought he had hurt you and that was all I needed to know. Now I feel bad about what I said."

Welcome to the club. "That's okay, Dad. Like I said, Virgil is not in a forgiving mood right now anyway."

"So there's no chance the two of you can patch things up and get back together?"

Kara shook her head as she recalled Virgil's words. *Without trust, love is nothing and you proved what we shared was nothing.*

"No, Dad. There's no way Virgil and I will ever get back together."

The finality of what she'd just said overwhelmed her and she knew she had to end the call with her father before he detected anything. "I've got a ton of things to do," she said softly. "Goodbye, Dad. I love you."

"I love you, too, cupcake."

It was only after he clicked off his phone and she clicked off hers that she gave in to her tears.

CHAPTER 5

"Mr. Bougard, Ms. Goshay is on the line for you."

Virgil tossed his pen down on his desk. "Thanks, Pam. Please put her through." When he heard the connecting click, he said, "Yes, Kara?"

"I told you I would contact you when I completed my action plan."

Yes, she had said that a week ago. He had pushed the thought of hearing from her out of his mind. At least he'd tried, but he had found himself thinking a lot about Kara whether he wanted to or not.

"I was wondering when we can meet," she added, interrupting his thoughts.

He checked the calendar on his desk. "I'm booked solid the rest of the week. It will have to be sometime next week." *Or the week after that,* he thought to himself. He was in no hurry to see Kara again.

"It's imperative that we meet this week,

Virgil. I got a call from your father yesterday for an update. At that time he expressed that he wanted me to present my plan to you ASAP. I told him that I would."

"Now you can go back and tell him that you tried," he said. "Like I said, my calendar is full this week. To be honest it's full next week, as well."

"And there's no way you can squeeze me in *this* week?"

He heard the annoyance in her voice and figured she thought he was deliberately being difficult. "No, sorry. Unless . . ." he said, studying his calendar again.

"Unless what?"

"Unless we make it a business dinner. That will work for me. How about for you?"

He heard the pause, which lasted a little too long to suit him. Now he was the one getting annoyed. "Look, Kara. My time is precious and right now you're wasting it. Will you be able to meet me for dinner tomorrow or not?" Virgil snapped.

"Yes, I'm available for a business dinner tomorrow," Kara snapped back.

"Good. My administrative assistant will call you later today with details as to where we will meet."

"Fine."

"Goodbye."

When Kara heard the click in her ear, she leaned back in her chair, and she clicked off her own phone. "And goodbye to you, too, Mr. Obnoxious." Of course he hadn't heard her comment but it still felt good making it.

A business dinner? Why couldn't he just add her to his schedule? He couldn't be *that* busy. She guessed that in a way she should be grateful. He probably would not have agreed to meet with her at all if she hadn't told him about the telephone call she'd received from his father. Matthew had made it clear he expected them to work together, grudgingly or otherwise. She had no problem doing so but couldn't speak for Virgil.

Kara sighed deeply. It was obvious he was being difficult already. It wouldn't be the first time she'd had to do an image makeover on an unenthusiastic client. She couldn't let that be a deterrent to what needed to be done. She had a job to do and she intended to do it.

Arriving early, Virgil chose a table in the back of the Goldenrod Restaurant mainly for two reasons. First, the table sat beside a huge window and on a clear day you could see the mountain peaks of Chimney Rock. And, second, the location gave him a good view of the restaurant's entrance. For some reason he wanted to see Kara before she saw him.

No one had to tell him that he hadn't been pleasant yesterday while talking to her on the phone. She had a tendency to bring out the worst in him and she had been the last person he'd wanted to converse with, business or otherwise. And then for her to mention his father had called her, literally reminding him he had to toe the line, had annoyed the hell out of him.

If Virgil didn't know better, he would think his father was trying to play his hand at matchmaking. After all, his parents had liked Kara a lot. But he did know better because the one thing Matthew Bougard didn't do was play games. His father was too no-nonsense for that. The only reason his dad had insisted on hiring Kara was because she was the best and had a stellar track record to prove it.

Virgil saw Kara the moment she walked into the restaurant and knew his biggest challenge would be her. If he hadn't known Kara and had glanced up and seen her for the first time, he would have had the same reaction he noticed several men in the restaurant having now. Kara Goshay wasn't just a beautiful woman, she was downright striking. Her entrance into any room drew stares from both men and women.

She was wearing an olive-green pencil skirt with a matching jacket and white blouse. Probably on any other person the colors would look drab, but on Kara they looked stunning. The skirt emphasized every single curve of her body as well as her long, gorgeous legs. Her hair was neatly tied up in a knot and he thought the style high-lighted the gracefulness of her neck and the long, dark lashes fanning her eyes.

He thought now the same thing he did the very first time he'd ever laid eyes on her. She was a woman about whom fantasies — the hot and steamy kind — were made. Evidently others thought so, as well, and Virgil couldn't help noticing several men shift in their seats, probably wondering if they would get the opportunity to meet her. Get to know her better. And that, Virgil thought, was the kicker. He already knew Kara, better than most. Knew more than he wanted to remember knowing. Like how she looked underneath her outfit, the location of that half-moon tattoo and all about that little mole on her backside.

He knew where those long legs began and especially where they ended. And he was well aware of those curves — intimately. Every single one of them. And the firm breasts under her blouse . . . he knew them, too. Very well. He knew how they felt in a man's hand and how they tasted in his mouth.

She glanced over in his direction and their gazes met, then held much too long to suit him. He sighed deeply and wished he could break the connection and look away, focus his attention on something or someone else, but he couldn't. He could only sit there and stare at the woman now walking toward him. Stare and remember. However, for some reason he wasn't thinking about what had torn them apart, but his mind was remembering things they'd done together, especially in the bedroom. After a hard day at work, the bedroom — either his or hers — had been their playground. And they'd played a lot. He could vividly remember all the positions they'd tried, the games they'd played and the talks they'd had. Sexual chemistry had a way of overpowering them whenever they were together, and heaven help him, he was feeling it now with every step she took toward him.

Virgil was beginning to see that suggesting a business dinner might not have been a smart thing to do. He should have found a way to work her into his workday schedule. He tried not to notice how her hand was clutching a leather briefcase — the same one he'd given her for her birthday. He was surprised she still had it. He could remember the night he'd given it to her and how she had thanked him. Just remembering how she'd thanked him made his lower body ache.

Of its own accord his gaze lowered to her legs again, and he couldn't help but remember the last time they'd made love. And how those same legs had flanked him, locked him between her thighs while she rode him hard. Damn. That should be the last thing he was remembering. What he should be thinking about was how Kara had caused him so much misery and pain.

With the latter thought flaming through his brain, he stood to pull out her chair for her, pasted a smile on his face and said in a tight voice, "Kara. Glad you could make it."

"Thanks," Kara said once she was seated across from him. She immediately picked up on his mood and knew it wasn't good. Just her luck it would be a carryover from yesterday.

She glanced around. "Nice place."

At least he hadn't chosen someplace where they'd dined before as a couple. This restaurant had recently opened and was part of the new development on this side of town. Since taking office as mayor of Charlotte, Morgan Steele had kept his campaign promise to grow the city by attracting new businesses and major corporations. While driving here she'd passed a huge medical technology complex as well as several communications firms.

But it wasn't the town or the restaurant she was focusing on right now. It was Virgil. And he was staring at her. "Is something wrong?" she asked him.

"No. Why do you ask?"

She shrugged. If he hadn't realized he'd been staring then she wouldn't be the one to enlighten him. "No reason."

Kara averted her eyes, looking down at the menu that had been placed in front of her. Moments later she glanced back up at him. "If it's okay with you, we can skip the meal and just discuss my action plan."

He frowned. "No, it's not okay with me. I skipped lunch and I'm hungry. Have you eaten something already?"

"No. I haven't eaten since breakfast."

"Then what's the problem?"

She could give him a list but decided the less he knew the better. "There's no problem, Virgil. I just don't want to take up any more of your time than necessary."

Virgil's penetrating stare deepened. "Trust

me, Kara. You won't take up my time, mainly because I wouldn't let you."

He caught the glare in her eyes as she stared at him and it didn't bother him one way or another to know she was irritated with him. In a way, it should. She had a job to do and he was well aware that his unpleasant attitude wasn't making it easy for her. But then why should he make anything easy for her?

Sighing deeply, he placed his menu down. Hadn't he decided last week that he needed to move on, and in order to do that he had to get beyond all this anger he had for her? He looked over at her. "Kara?"

She glanced over at him. "Yes?"

"That apology you made six months ago. I accept it."

For a minute she didn't say anything but continued to stare at him. "I'm curious as to why you've decided to accept it now," she finally said.

He shrugged. "That shouldn't be so hard to figure out. We need to work together."

"And can we try to be friends?"

"No, I wouldn't go that far. I doubt we'll ever be friends. Forgiving does not mean forgetting."

She narrowed her gaze at him. "Then why bother?"

"Do you prefer I not accept your apology?"

She rolled her eyes. "Do whatever you want to do, Virgil. I don't care anymore."

He really didn't care that she didn't care. "Now that I've accepted your apology, let's decide what we're having for dinner."

After giving the waiter her order, Kara took a sip of her ice water. While Virgil was telling the waiter what he wanted for dinner, she took time to think about his acceptance of her apology.

Did he honestly assume she believed just saying he accepted her apology meant his attitude toward her would change? She knew better and like she'd told him, she really didn't care.

So why are you letting it bother you if you don't care? a voice inside her head asked.

"So how are things going at the office, Kara?"

The sound of his husky voice intruded into her thoughts. Why was he asking her that as if he really cared? However, since he was making an attempt to be civil, she would tell him. "Everything is going fine. Cassandra no longer works for me. She and Eric moved to San Diego to be closer to his family. That way she could get help with the baby."

Cassandra was the young woman who'd been her administrative assistant during the time they'd been a couple. But Cassandra had been more than just an employee, she had been her friend, as well. Cassandra and Eric had been two of the first people she'd met upon moving to Charlotte. The couple had lived in a condo a few doors down. Kara had been looking for office help at the same time Cassandra's job had been downsized.

"Baby? Cassandra had a baby?"

Kara couldn't help the smile that touched her lips. "Yes, a beautiful little girl named Regan. Regan is about two years old now."

Virgil smiled and Kara knew this smile was genuine. "I'm happy for her."

"So am I." Kara knew he would be happy for Cassandra because her former administrative assistant would bend the rules for Virgil. Like allowing him to sneak into her office when she was away to leave special notes on her desk, drop breakfast off for her or personally deliver her flowers . . . no matter how many times she would tell Cassandra she didn't want to be disturbed. And Kara would also admit Cassandra had been the one person who hadn't believed Marti's lie about Virgil.

She banished the thought from her mind. She was here for a business dinner, she reminded herself, so best to get to business. "I sent copies of my proposed action plan to both you and Matthew. I assume you looked over it."

"Can't speak for Dad but I haven't had the chance. So please enlighten me. What kind of strategies did you come up with, Kara?"

She wished there wasn't a tingling sensation that moved up her spine each and every time he said her name. Leaning back in her seat, she said, "Usually when I take on a client, I have three areas to concentrate on for improvement. What I consider the ABC's. Appearance, behavior and communication. There's nothing wrong with the way you dress and your communication skills are excellent. That means we need to zero in on your behavior."

"What do you suggest?"

"I note that, although your company is involved in a lot of worthwhile causes and is a huge benefactor to a number of charitable organizations, you're rarely seen supporting them."

He frowned. "I beg to differ. Just last week I was seen at that banquet for cancer research."

"Yes, you were. It was a black-tie affair. What about the cancer walk?"

"What about it?"

"You didn't participate in that. Your senior and junior executives did but you didn't. You only make appearances at the galas and balls, as if to court your clients there. You never appear where people in the community can see you, get to know you."

When he didn't say anything, she pressed on. "My recommendation is for you to be seen at a lot more of those types of events. Several of the major corporations around town will be getting together for a back-to-school extravaganza. I believe your company will be giving away book bags. I suggest you put in an appearance there instead of sending one of your executives."

Again, he didn't say anything, as if mulling over her suggestion. "Okay, I can do that."

"And there's a 5k walk for cancer research next month. I suggest you sign up for that, as well."

"Fine. Prepare a list of such activities you think I should participate in and pass the information on to my administrative assistant to add to my calendar."

Her next recommendation wouldn't go

over so well with him. "I did my research and you've garnered quite a reputation around town with women."

She quickly held up her hand. "And before you try giving me that same spiel you gave your father about being single and dating whomever you please and not being accountable to anyone, you might want to rethink that assumption."

"Why should I?" he asked coolly.

"Because your image as a womanizer is hurting your company. It's giving Marv Hilton the ammunition he needs to make you seem worse than you really are. I agree that as a single, unattached bachelor you should be free to date whomever and whenever you want. However, to curtail what Hilton is saying, you need to tone down your social life."

"What do you mean 'tone down my social life'?"

"I strongly suggest that, for the next few months, you're seen around town with the same woman and no one else."

CHAPTER 6

Virgil's glacier-cold eyes narrowed. "That's not going to happen. There's no way I'll establish an exclusive relationship with any woman. Ever again." And he figured she knew the reason why. She had been the first and the last woman he'd claim exclusivity with and look where it had gotten him.

"It won't be permanent, Virgil. You've dated a lot of women over the years. I'm sure there's one you wouldn't mind being seen with for a while on a regular basis."

"There's not a single one. Besides, I don't want to give any one of them ideas that our relationship might one day go somewhere."

"Then we can hire a woman from a legitimate escort service. I happen to know someone who owns such a discreet company out of DC. She only hires educated women, some who speak several languages. They are poised, classy, sophisticated and —"

"No. There has to be another way. I just

won't date as many women as I've done in the past."

She shook her head. "In order for this plan to work, Virgil, you will need to restrict yourself to being seen with one woman. It's a lifestyle change you temporarily need to make. Men feel threatened by you and want to keep their wives, sisters and daughters away from you. Some of those same men are potential clients. Is that what you want?"

"No. Hilton has become a pain in the ass that I plan to take care of."

Kara lifted a brow. "Take care of how?"

"Two can play his games."

"What do you mean?"

"I'm using York's investigative firm to dig into Whitney Hilton's past. Like I said. Two can play Hilton's game." Marv Hilton hadn't known the mistake he was making by messing with him. Virgil had never hesitated to retaliate before and he certainly wouldn't now.

"Digging up information on Whitney might serve your purpose of stopping Hilton from spreading his lies, but it won't help the issue of your image. You need to do something now even if it's nothing but a temporary fix."

He leaned in to make his point clearer. "Dating any woman exclusively for any amount of time is out of the question." He sat back when the waiter brought their meals and quickly departed.

"All I'm saying, Virgil, is you should think about my suggestion."

He picked up his fork and put an end to the conversation. "There's nothing to think about."

Virgil had finished his steak before he noticed conversation between him and Kara was nonexistent. And he was okay with that. He'd needed to gather himself anyway. As much as he didn't want them to, memories of other times they'd shared a meal were nearly suffocating him. Granted they'd never dined at this particular restaurant, but there had been others.

He glanced over at her and saw she was looking everywhere but at him as she ate. That was fine because he had no problem looking at her. And he did so as he took a leisurely sip of his drink. A spike of intense awareness shot up his spine. He wasn't surprised by the sudden reaction, just a little annoyed. How could he still desire a woman who'd hurt him the way she had? Slowly inhaling a deep breath, he drew her scent into his nostrils and the lower part of his gut ached with the familiar scent. And why was he concentrating on her lips?

She glanced over at him and caught him staring. She didn't say anything for a minute and then she smiled and asked, "How are your godbrothers?"

Virgil placed his glass down. Her smile was unexpected and for a quick second it threw him off-kilter. He rebounded quickly.

"Everyone is fine. Even the married ones."

"Why wouldn't they be? Even the married ones?"

"No reason."

"They seem happy."

He lifted a brow. "You've seen them with their wives?"

She shrugged and his gaze moved to her shoulders. He recalled the times he had kissed those shoulders and how they had felt beneath his lips and hands.

"Only from a distance," she said. "At that party six months ago."

Virgil nodded. "Yes, they are happy and I am happy for them. They married good women." He figured he would leave it at that, deciding not to add that his godbrothers had married women who trusted them. A hell of a lot more than she'd trusted him.

"And how are your parents?" he asked, trying not to recall the last time he'd spoken to her father and the names the man had called him.

"They're fine. In fact I talked to Dad last week. I hadn't known he'd called you when we broke up. He said he tried calling to apologize but couldn't reach you. You'd changed your number."

"Yes, I changed it." He didn't explain that he did it to end all ties with her.

"Yes, well . . . Dinner was great, Virgil. I hope we were able to agree on a number of things."

"We did. Once my personal assistant provides me with that list of events you prepare, I'll see how many I can add to my calendar." He gestured to the waiter for the check, then turned back to her. "As far as the other suggestion, I think there has to be another way, so cross that one off your list."

Virgil had barely made it inside his condo when his cell phone rang. It was Xavier. "Yes, X?" he asked after clicking on the line.

"Just checking in with everyone about next month when Winston comes home. He's arriving a week before the party so all of us can hang out. You game?"

"Yes," Virgil replied, pulling the tie from around his neck and removing his jacket. "Zion and I should be asking if you, W, Y and U are game since you four are married

86

and have to check in with your wives."

"Don't be a smart-ass, V."

There was a pause and then Xavier asked, "So what's this I hear about your company hiring Kara to do an image makeover for you?"

Since he hadn't mentioned it to anyone but Winston, he figured Winston must have mentioned it to the others. "It was Dad's idea."

"Um, makes perfect sense. She's good at what she does. Cameron has used her firm to do group training for his employees on more than one occasion. He thought she did a fantastic job. Has she come up with a game plan?"

Cameron Cody was the founder and CEO of Cody Enterprises. Xavier was not only the executive attorney for Cody, he was considered Cameron's right-hand man and the two were very close friends. "Yes, she came up with a game plan," Virgil said, kicking off his shoes. "Her recommendation that I become more visible around town during charity events is doable."

"You do that already."

"Not to the extent she thinks that I should. I do a lot of black-tie affairs. I'm never seen walking marathons for charities or in the soup kitchens helping to feed the homeless.

She thinks that's a good way to improve my image in the community."

"I agree. Cameron and the Steeles are always visible that way. It's good PR. There're a lot of new businesses moving to town, and when they're new to the area and want to size you up, their best level of measurement is how well you're thought of in the community. What else did she recommend?"

"The other thing she suggested is something I won't go along with."

"And what's that?"

"To began dating exclusively for a while to give the impression that my bachelor days are winding down."

"That might not be a bad idea, V. If you did that then you'll appear to be more focused on your company and not so much on seducing women."

Virgil put the phone on speaker as he removed his shirt, frowning. "I'm a single man with a healthy appetite for women, X. Why should I change my routine?"

Xavier's deep chuckle sounded through the phone. "Healthy appetite for women? Admit it, V, since your breakup with Kara you've taken the word *player* to a whole other level. Granted, you're up front with the women and let them know you're not into anything serious, but still, you're out there quite a bit. It's like you're afraid to give another woman the time and attention you gave Kara."

"I'm not afraid, just cautious. Once you get burned you're smart enough not to play with fire again." He picked up the phone again. "Anyway, I offered Kara a compromise."

"What was your compromise?"

"That instead of dating one woman exclusively, I decrease the number of women I'm seeing."

"What did she think of that?"

"I could tell she wasn't thrilled with the idea."

For a moment Xavier was quiet, and then he said, "Do me a favor, V, and let Kara do her job. I agree with her that total exclusivity would work better in your case, especially with that Hilton guy trying to be an ass. Fathers get real crazy when it comes to their daughters. In this case the justification for the craziness isn't there, but still. We all agree you need to clean up your act for a while. You're not talking about forever."

"Forever or not, like I told Kara, there's not a woman I can start seeing steadily who won't get crazy ideas she might become permanent. I'd rather not deal with that kind of foolishness."

"I know just the woman who might fit your needs. You've dated her before and the two of you hit it off. You won't have to worry about her getting any crazy ideas and she's definitely a looker."

Xavier had piqued Virgil's curiosity as well as his interest. "Who is she, man?"

"Kara."

Virgil nearly dropped the mobile phone out of his hand. "Kara? Are you crazy? Why in the hell would I want to start seeing Kara again? For any reason?"

"Dammit, V, I'm right here. You don't have to yell. What are you trying to do? Destroy my eardrums?"

"Better than getting in my car and going to your place to kick your ass."

"Calm down and think about it, V. First of all, according to you, there will never be anything between you and Kara again."

"There won't be."

"In that case, what are you worrying about? Kara is a well-respected and well-liked young woman in the community, who also happens to be a savvy businesswoman. When people see you together, they will think it was a smart move on your part. And like I said, she's a looker so it will squash any man's notion that you'd be after his wife, sisters or daughters. There wouldn't be a need when you have a woman like Kara who has both looks and brains. Besides, the two of you know it's only for show, to clean up your image. You don't have to worry about Kara getting any designs on you or you on her."

Virgil knew Xavier had made some valid points. But . . . "I don't know, X. I could barely tolerate being with her at dinner tonight."

"Why? You claim you don't feel anything for her."

"And I don't. I finally told her tonight that I accept her apology. But before you get any crazy ideas about me and Kara rekindling anything, forget it. I'm telling you the same thing I told her. Forgiving doesn't mean forgetting."

"It should. You need to forgive and forget, V."

"Don't think that I can. She believed her sister's lie."

"We all make mistakes. Farrah doesn't have a sister but she and Natalie are best friends. Had Natalie told Farrah she saw me checking into a hotel with another woman, I can bet you Farrah would have believed her."

Farrah was Xavier's beautiful wife and

regardless of what he said, Virgil knew she would not have believed her husband guilty of being unfaithful. "Kara should have known I would not have cheated on her. Hell, I gave up that lifestyle for her and gave her no reason to think I would be unfaithful. I loved her, X."

Virgil wasn't sure why he was trying to convince Xavier of anything. He'd had similar conversations with all his godbrothers. They had liked Kara and felt he'd been too hard on her.

"Kara loves her sister and she had no idea what Marti was capable of doing. Fortunately, I did. If you recall, Marti and I dated for three weeks. That's all the time it took for me to see Marti Goshay was bad news. I honestly think she has this thing against men."

Virgil shook his head. "I can't believe you'd suggest Kara as the woman I should be seen with exclusively."

"Think about it. It would sure piss Marti off royally if she thought you and Kara had gotten back together. It would serve her right."

Yes, it would, Virgil thought. Whenever he had run into Marti she'd smiled at him as though she'd taken great pleasure in ruining things between him and Kara. To this day Virgil didn't have a clue as to why. How could one sibling do something like that to another? It was crazy.

"Now that I think about it, you and Kara as a couple might not be a good idea after all," Xavier said.

Virgil lifted a brow. "Why?"

"You might run the risk of falling for her again."

"That won't happen."

"It might."

"It won't, X. I could never love Kara again." There was no need to tell his god-brother that the only thing he felt whenever he saw Kara was lust. The same degree of lust that he felt for any other good-looking woman.

Virgil glanced at his watch. His favorite television show would be on soon. "I need to go, X. I'll talk to you later."

"Hey, wait! There's a reason I called."

"It better be good. You've wasted twenty minutes of my time already talking about that Kara foolishness."

"It's good," Xavier said chuckling. "Farrah and I are having another baby."

CHAPTER 7

Frowning in irritation, Virgil stepped off the elevator to the executive floor of Bougard Enterprises. Why had he allowed Xavier to put that foolish notion into his head about Kara stepping into the role of his exclusive love interest? And what bothered him more than anything was that he'd been giving it serious consideration. How crazy was that?

He hadn't been able to sit and watch his favorite TV show for thinking about the possibilities . . . especially how the thought that he and Kara were back together would irk Marti to no end. But what really had him twitching in the gut was his attraction to Kara. Last night's dinner showed she could still raise his desire to an unprecedented level. It had taken every bit of control he had to concentrate on the taste of his steak and not allow his mind to be flooded with memories of the taste of her.

However, like Xavier had pointed out,

such a move had its advantages. But just like there were pluses, he could think of several minuses.

He walked into the lobby adjacent to his office. "Good morning, Pam."

His administrative assistant gave him a huge smile. "Good morning, Mr. Bougard. Your father is waiting for you in your office."

Virgil's smile faded. "He is?"

"Yes."

Virgil assumed his parents would stay in Houston for at least another month. In addition to Leigh and Chad, his father's family still lived there as well as a few high school pals he'd stayed close to over the years. That was one of the reasons his parents had purchased a second home in Houston.

"Hold my calls for a while, Pam."

"Sure thing."

He walked into his office to find his father standing at the window staring out. "Dad, I hadn't expected you back in Charlotte for a while."

His father turned around and smiled. "And I hadn't expected to come back. Rhona remembered she agreed to be commencement speaker next weekend at UNC Charlotte. She wanted to return early to concentrate on writing her speech."

"I see." Virgil wondered if that meant his father would be hanging around Bougard Enterprises while he was in town. His father's next words gave him hope that would not be the case.

"Rhona suggested I fly back to Houston tomorrow. A few of the guys — former high school classmates of mine — planned a fishing trip this weekend." Matthew chuckled. "Your mother needs to work on her speech and claims I'll be a distraction if I am here."

"And I agree," Virgil said smiling. "You know how quiet Mom likes it when she's in her Dr. Rhona B. Bougard mode, Dad."

In all honesty, Virgil was proud of his mother, who had earned her PhD in education before he had started high school. She had been the president of Johnson C. Smith University for years before retiring two years ago.

Matthew nodded. "I definitely don't want to distract Rhona and there's really no reason to hang around here. I got a copy of Kara's action plan. It seems the two of you have everything under control."

Virgil moved toward his desk to place his briefcase on top of it. If his father assumed that was the case then he would let him. "I take it you looked over what she proposed."

"Yes. Her recommendations are on point. I can see how they will improve your image. Having a steady woman and making yourself more visible in the community where it counts are good strategies."

Virgil figured now was not the time to tell his father that, although he intended to be more visible in the community, he had no intention of having a steady woman of any kind.

"Well, I'll be going now. I'm flying back to Houston tomorrow for that fishing trip." Before heading for the door Matthew said, "I'll see you when I get back next week, and I'm looking forward to meeting your lady."

Virgil raised a brow. "What lady?"

"The one you select to be seen around town with on a consistent basis. And it would be nice if you brought her to UNCC's commencement to hear your mom's speech. I anticipate a lot of people will be there and it will be a great place to be seen with her. For you to bring her around your parents will give the impression the two of you are serious."

Matthew glanced at his watch. "I need to run. Can't keep my queen waiting." And then he opened the door and was gone.

Virgil sat down at his desk and stared at the closed door for a long moment while thinking that some days it didn't pay to get out of bed. He built a steeple with his fingers while leaning back in deep thought. His father naturally assumed he would fall in line with every one of Kara's recommendations since he expected his son to put the needs of Bougard Enterprises before his own.

Virgil knew there was no good reason for him not to go along with everything Kara had suggested. And taking everything into consideration, he also knew Xavier was right. Kara would be the logical choice if he did so.

He stood, walked over to the window and shoved his hands in his pockets as he looked out. How would she feel if he suggested such a thing? For all he knew she was already in a relationship with someone. He hadn't made it his business to keep tabs on her since their breakup. As far as he'd been concerned, the less he knew about what was going on with her, the better.

He had to admit that rekindling an affair with Kara would seem more believable to people than for him to suddenly develop a deep interest in one of his lovers. Why did the thought of having to spend so much time with Kara twist his insides into knots? Considering their strained relationship, could the two of them even pull such a thing off?

His cell phone rang and from the ringtone he knew it was York. He and his wife Darcy lived in New York. Pulling the phone out of his pocket, he clicked it on. "Yes, Y?"

"Just giving you an update. I've been gathering information on Whitney Hilton's past as you requested, but you might want me to take a look at her old man's, as well."

"Marv Hilton? Why?"

"I'm finding stuff on him that's rather interesting."

Virgil nodded. "Interesting enough to use as leverage to make him back off?"

"Possibly. He's a businessman. One who's well thought of in the community. I'm sure he wouldn't want anything from his past to resurface that could tarnish his image like he's trying to do to yours. What's the saying? Don't try cleaning up somebody else's house unless yours is spotless."

"I see what you mean. Let's see what we can find that could possibly stop him in his tracks."

"Will do."

After hanging up the phone, Virgil leaned back against the windowsill. If York was to find some damaging information on old man Hilton, then . . .

Virgil knew he couldn't get his hopes up on that possibility. Even if York was onto something, it might take weeks before Virgil received a final report. So he was back to square one. The action plan Kara had devised.

He knew what he had to do. Drawing in a deep sigh he walked back over to his desk and picked up his phone. "Yes, Mr. Bougard?"

"Pam, please get Kara Goshay on the line."

Kara looked up from her documents. "Yes, Janice?"

"Someone is here to see you and he doesn't have an appointment."

Kara raised an arched brow. "Who is it?"

From the tone of Janice's voice, it was apparent whoever had dropped by without an appointment was standing within listening range of their conversation.

"Mr. Virgil Bougard and he says he needs to speak with you immediately."

Kara frowned. Virgil had called twice today already, but at the time, she hadn't had the inclination to talk to him and had told Janice to tell him that she would call him back by the end of the day. She'd taken as much of him as she could at dinner last night. Dealing with him had left her emotionally drained and she wondered what was so important for him to seek her out today.

"Okay, Janice, please send him in."

Kara stood, not wanting to remember Virgil's last visit to her office and all the scandalous things they had done in here. It had taken months, or rather years, to wipe the memories from her mind and the last thing she needed was for them to resurface. But they were doing so anyway.

She had been working late one night and Virgil had surprised her with takeout dinner. She would never forget the moment she had looked up from the stack of papers on her desk to find him standing there with a delivery bag in his hand. The aroma of the food had gotten to her, but it was the look of heated desire in his eyes that had really set everything inside her throbbing.

She wasn't sure how they got through their meal. Needless to say, after finishing off the food, they had then proceeded to finish off each other. She wasn't sure who'd made the first move that night, nor had she cared. The main thing she remembered was that they'd both stripped naked and made out all over this room. After that night she hadn't been able to sit down at her desk and not remember the time he'd made love to her on top of it.

The door opened and Virgil walked in. Her breath caught with every step he took into the room. He had a serious expression on his face but that wasn't the primary thing holding her attention. As usual he was male perfection, immaculately dressed and handsome as sin. She really didn't like the way her body was responding to him and fought hard for control.

She watched Virgil close the door behind himself and glance over at her. "Thanks for seeing me, Kara."

Coming around her desk, she leaned back against the front of it. "What's this visit about, Virgil? What's so urgent that it couldn't wait until I could return your call later today?"

He shoved his hands into his pockets. "I've changed my mind."

She lifted a brow. "Changed your mind about what?"

"Your recommendation that I date a woman exclusively."

She was definitely surprised to hear this. But she also knew him well enough to know there was something more to it than him having a mere change of heart. "What made you change your mind?"

He didn't say anything for a moment. It

was as if he needed to make sure whatever words he spoke were given much thought. "I realized nothing is more important to me than Bougard Enterprises, and that I would do just about anything to ensure its continued success. Even if it means making sacrifices."

She nodded. "I think you're making the right decision. And like I said yesterday, if you're not comfortable with dating someone you know already, I have a friend who owns a legitimate escort service. One that has a good reputation for being discreet. I can call —"

"That's not necessary. I have someone in mind."

She really shouldn't be surprised that he did, although he'd claimed otherwise yesterday. "Fine. Then I'll let you take care of that part of things. You don't need me for that."

"Oh, but I will need you."

She was confused. "Why would you?"

He crossed the room to stand in front of her. "Mainly because I want *you* to be that woman. The one I will be dating exclusively."

CHAPTER 8

Kara stared at him. She figured he had to be joking but the intense look in his eyes indicated he was dead serious. And considering his attitude at dinner last night and the things he'd said, that made her angry. "You have some nerve coming here and suggesting something like that. If I remember correctly, although you accepted my apology, you made it clear you would never forget about what I accused you of. You stated without batting an eye that we could never be friends. And I know the only reason you're even tolerating me is because of Matthew."

"Will you at least hear me out?"

She raised her chin. "Why should I?"

"Because I'm the client, and although you presented my company with a good action plan, there's an aspect of it that won't work unless modifications are made."

She narrowed her gaze at him. "I will work

with any modifications you suggest as long as they don't include me."

"But they do include you, because this idea of yours can only work with you."

She rolled her eyes. "That's the most ridiculous thing I've ever heard. Why on earth would you, of all people, think that?"

"Because it's true. I will only feel comfortable with a woman that I know for certain won't get any ideas. You won't, since you know our relationship will never go back to the way it was before. And you know the arrangement is strictly a strategy to improve my image. I prefer not sharing such personal details with anyone else."

"And you wouldn't have to if we used that escort service that I told you about."

"It's too risky. What if someone was to discover it's nothing but a sham and that I'm paying someone to be seen with me?" He held up his hand when she opened her mouth to speak. "Before you say that there's no way anyone will ever find out, think again. Even with all the precautions and safeguards you put in place, can you guarantee that won't happen, Kara? Think about the consequences if it does. That would be a scandal Bougard Enterprises could never recover from."

Kara knew he was right, but —

He cut off her thoughts. "Your company was hired to fix my image, Kara, not make a bigger mess of it."

Virgil's words momentarily froze Kara and she held his gaze with her glare. "I know what my company was hired to do and I know what I'm doing, Virgil. Don't treat me like I don't."

She saw the agitation in his face when he said, "Bougard Enterprises would not have hired you if we didn't believe that you knew what you're doing, trust me. All I'm saying is that for this plan of yours to work, all players have to be in the game. I know what I'm capable of doing and I doubt I can pretend interest in some woman."

"But you can pretend interest in me? Knowing how you feel about me, that doesn't make sense," she countered.

"Think about it, Kara. It makes perfect sense. First of all, you and I have a history and a lot of people remember that history. When they see us together again they will assume we've worked out whatever differences kept us apart."

He paused a moment then added, "And as far as pretending interest in you, that will be easy, because that's all it will be — pretense. And I won't have to worry about you getting the wrong idea about anything."

Kara hated admitting it but everything he'd said was true. They had dated exclusively for a full year and had been known as a couple in the community. They'd gone to events together and were always seen together. Everyone had speculated that eventually a wedding date would be announced. Some had even considered them the darling couple of Charlotte. At least that's how the society pages had pegged them thanks to a popular news column called *Flo on the Ro.*

For some reason the editor, a woman by the name of Florence Asbury, a romantic at heart, enjoyed keeping readers abreast on the romantic lives of some of Charlotte's prominent singles. Originally her column was called *Flo on the Romance Scene,* but later the title was shortened and became known as *Flo on the Ro.* Flo enlisted what had become known as Flo's Posse and the group would roam around town keeping their eyes and ears open for any newsworthy romantic gossip. A few years ago Flo and her posse had decided Kara and Virgil were newsworthy and she enjoyed writing about them in her weekly column, which had quite a following.

Then their breakup happened and it had fueled rumors as to what had caused it. It didn't help matters when Virgil reverted back to his old ways of being Charlotte's number-one womanizer.

"And you honestly believe people will assume we've reconciled our differences and are back together?" she asked him.

"I don't see why not. They only speculated as to why we broke up. Besides, it doesn't matter. It's been years and people love a good make-up story."

Although Kara knew that to be true, she just wasn't sure that she and Virgil should be in the starring roles of one. He indicated he could pretend, but could she? And why should she? She wasn't responsible for his less-than-stellar image. However, she had been hired to fix it. And for that reason, a part of her refused to let his company be the one she failed to make into another success story. But still . . .

"I have to think about this, Virgil. There has to be another way."

"If there is, you need to come up with it by next weekend. Mom is keynote speaker at UNCC's graduation and Dad wants me to bring whatever woman I've decided to date exclusively. He figures it will be the perfect time for us to be seen together."

Kara agreed with Matthew that it would be the perfect time — if the plans didn't include her. "Like I said, I have to think about it. I'll get back in touch with you."

He nodded and, without saying anything else, he turned and walked out of her office.

"So let me get this straight," Cassandra Gilbert said to Kara through the phone line. "You found out Marti lied so you apologized to Virgil. He didn't accept your apology at first but has since come around, although grudgingly. And now his image needs repairing because of some scandal with another woman. Your company has been hired to fix it. And in doing so you'll be presented as his exclusive love interest."

"Yes, that's about it," Kara responded, setting her wineglass on her coffee table. She had needed someone to talk to and couldn't wait to get home to call her friend.

"In a way it's a rather smart move. Everyone will simply think the two of you have made up and gotten back together."

"That's the plan."

"Okay, so what's the problem?"

Kara rolled her eyes. "We're talking about Virgil Bougard, Cassandra."

"I know who we're talking about, and the way I see it, there shouldn't be a problem unless . . ."

"Unless what?"

"Unless you're not as indifferent to him

as you claim you are."

Kara frowned. "What do you mean by that?"

"I think you know what I mean, Kara. You loved Virgil too much not to feel anything for him now."

"Have you forgotten that I thought he betrayed me? When that happened, I stopped loving him," Kara reminded her.

"Yes, I know how hurt you were, but did you really stop loving him?"

"Of course I did. I moved on."

"Moved on? Who are you trying to fool? You never allowed yourself to get seriously involved with anyone else. Yes, you dated after Virgil but you never let anyone get close. I was there, Kara. I know. Besides, Virgil isn't a man a woman can fall out of love with easily."

Kara defended herself. "Considering that I thought Virgil had betrayed me, falling out of love with him would have been understandable."

"Understandable, yes, but it would not have been you. Like I said, you loved Virgil too much. You were hurt, devastated, but you can't convince me that you fell out of love with him completely."

Kara wanted to argue with her friend, but Cassandra moved on to another topic. "I just can't believe Marti did that to you."

"Sometimes I can't believe it myself. I probably would never have found out if I hadn't overheard that phone call."

"Did she say why she did it?"

"She claims she was looking out for my best interests and felt Virgil would have eventually hurt me."

"That's crazy. Virgil loved you. Anybody could see that. I guess that's one of the reasons I never thought he was guilty even when you did."

Kara drew in a deep breath. "And now he hates me."

"I doubt if he could hate you, Kara."

"Trust me, he does. I can see it in his eyes whenever he looks at me."

"Yet he wants the two of you to pretend to be lovers?"

"Only to serve a purpose," Kara said drily.

"So what are you going to do?"

"I don't know. It's my proposed action plan that he's using. I just didn't think he would involve me personally. I'll sleep on it and hopefully I will make the right decision tomorrow."

"If I were in your shoes do you know what I would do?"

A part of Kara was afraid to ask. "What?"

"I would use that opportunity with Virgil

to your advantage and remind him why he fell in love with you in the first place. I would make him remember how good the two of you were together."

Kara shook her head even though her friend couldn't see her. "I'm not even sure I wish that was possible."

"Regardless of what you're saying, I believe you and Virgil should be together. Your love just needs rekindling. A love as strong as the two of you had will never die."

Kara wasn't as convinced as Cassandra seemed to be. "He's changed. It's like his heart is made of ice and it's my fault for not trusting him."

"If his heart has turned to ice then you owe it to yourself to melt it."

Kara fought back her tears. "I honestly don't think I can."

"And I believe that you can. There's something you've omitted from your action plan, Kara. It's the only thing that can really help improve Virgil's image and behavior permanently. It will require that you and Virgil work out your differences and get back together for real. Otherwise, all you'll be doing is applying a temporary fix to the problem. Virgil might not know it, but he needs you back in his life. You were able to change him for the better once before and I believe you can do it again. The man loved you. He was happy back then. You owe it to yourself . . . and to him . . . to make him happy again."

Cassandra's words echoed in Kara's thoughts long after they'd said goodbye. Later that night after she had taken her shower and slid between the sheets, Kara couldn't stop thinking about everything Cassandra had said. Her friend was such an optimist, yet . . . *If his heart has turned to ice then you owe it to yourself to melt it.*

Cassandra was right on point about the changes Virgil had made after they'd begun dating. When she'd met Virgil, he'd had a reputation of getting any woman he wanted. Yet she had made him earn his way into her bed. His entire outlook on life had changed and she knew for certain he'd given up his entourage of women just to be with her. She had been his one and only . . . until Marti's lie had made her believe otherwise.

And now he was back to his old womanizing ways. And she of all people was hired to clean up his image. Cassandra was right. All her company would do was put a bandage on the problem and not provide a permanent solution. It would be just a matter of time before he resorted back to his womanizing ways.

Could she be Virgil's permanent solution as Cassandra thought?

By the time sleep had lulled her to close her eyes, she had at least admitted something to herself. She was still in love with Virgil Bougard.

CHAPTER 9

"Mr. Bougard, Kara Goshay is —"

"Put her call through," he interrupted.

He hoped Kara had made a decision about what he'd proposed to her yesterday, especially after he read the article appearing in that morning's newspaper. And then there was the phone call he'd received from Thomas Fortner.

Fortner had informed Virgil that he was considering taking his business elsewhere after playing golf with Marv Hilton this weekend. Virgil could just imagine what embellishment Hilton had added to the story to make Fortner consider doing such a thing.

"Ms. Goshay is not on the phone, sir. She's here and would like to see you."

Kara was here? "Please send her in."

He clicked off the phone and adjusted his tie as he stood. In the old days Kara rarely read the morning paper before noon so chances were she was unaware of the article. In that case, was she here to turn down what he'd suggested yesterday? Fearing that possibility, last night he'd tried coming up with a plan B and had even gone so far as to make a list of other women. Not a single one he'd considered a strong candidate.

The door to his office opened and Kara walked in. He wondered if there would ever be a time when her entrance into any room would not take his breath away. As usual she looked beautiful. Professional and sexy rolled into one. Her chocolate-brown business suit emphasized her small waist and curvy hips. However, it was what was beneath that business suit that he was remembering so well.

It wasn't even ten in the morning, yet she looked as radiant as any woman had a right to be this early. She had a graceful, fluid walk, something he'd always admired watching, and he wasn't surprised at the sexual chemistry that surrounded them. It had always been that way and always would, regardless of how they barely tolerated each other.

"Kara, to what do I owe this visit?" He studied her. There was something about her that looked different this morning and he wasn't sure what it was.

"I've made a decision regarding your request yesterday. The one about us dating exclusively just for show."

"And?"

"And like you said, there could never be anything between us again. But letting people assume there is might work in our favor. Your image will improve and I'll get another success story to boast about."

So in essence she would be using him like he would be using her. Why did the thought of that bother him? There was no reason for it. Like she said, in the end both of them would benefit.

"Are you willing to attend that commencement with me next weekend?" he asked her.

"Yes. I'm sure your father will explain things to your mother so she'll know the truth."

"I'm sure he will." He paused a minute then asked, "This plan will also require us to be seen together on occasion, around town, having dinners, going to movies. Do you have a problem with that?"

"I should be asking you that, Virgil. Will you have a problem with us being seen as if we're getting back together?"

Virgil knitted his brow for a second as he contemplated. "No, I won't have a problem with it. Those I care about will know the truth."

"Fine. Then I'll see you next weekend," she said, turning to leave.

"Meet with me later today."

She turned back around. "Why?"

"To plan our strategy. Did you see the newspaper this morning?"

"No."

He picked up the copy off his desk and handed it to her. "We've drawn interest already."

Kara read the headlines in the *Flo on the Ro* column.

Has Charlotte's Biggest Womanizer Finally Come to His Senses?

Virgil Bougard was seen having dinner last week with Kara Goshay. It's been almost four years and the big question on this editor's mind is . . . are these two on again? I certainly hope so and think it's about time. Stay tuned.

A frown bunched Kara's brows. Below the article was a photo of her and Virgil enjoying dinner together that day at the Goldenrod Restaurant. Shaking her head, she handed the paper back to Virgil. "Who took that picture?"

118

"No telling. Smartphones can turn anyone into a photographer these days. Now we have to deal with everyone speculating. For us that might be a good thing. We need to keep the momentum going by being seen together often."

"We'll be seen together next weekend at UNCC's commencement ceremony."

"I think a couple of times before then wouldn't hurt. Let's meet later to discuss it. Plan strategies."

Kara was inwardly elated he'd suggested meeting with her later; especially after she'd awakened that morning to decide Cassandra's suggestion last night had merit. She would use this opportunity to remind Virgil how good things used to be between them. Even if it didn't work, she felt it was a risk worth taking. The key was to not let him suspect anything, which meant she couldn't appear too eager for them to spend time together.

She gave a half-hearted protest. "I have a full day today, Virgil. I'm not sure I'll have time later."

His eyes narrowed. She could tell he didn't like to be denied. He was a man who was used to getting whatever he wanted. "I suggest you squeeze me in somehow, Kara."

She held his gaze and wondered what was

there in the penetrating depths staring back at her. Cockiness? Anger? Lust? She hadn't missed the latter when she'd entered his office. He might be mad at her but she had clearly seen lust in his eyes when she'd arrived. That had given her hope. "Fine," she finally said. "We can meet somewhere later this evening. Have your administrative assistant call and —"

"I will be the one who calls you," he said, taking his phone out of his pocket. "What's your number?"

"It didn't change."

He nodded and then punched in her phone number. She couldn't help being pleased that he remembered it. When her cell phone rang, he said, "Now you have my new number. Use it to reach me if you need to."

"I doubt I will." Turning back toward the door, she was surprised to hear him say, "You never know." Then she walked out.

When the door closed shut behind Kara, Virgil sat down at his desk and leaned back in his chair. He'd figured out what was different about her today. Her hair. It still hung to her shoulders but instead of being curly it was straight. He always liked the curly hair style on her but thought he liked this one even better.

He then frowned. The fact that he'd noticed such a thing didn't sit well with him. Why would it matter to him one iota how she wore her hair? But he couldn't help remembering those times he would run his fingers through the thick strands and how he would enjoy gripping a handful of her hair whenever they made love.

He muttered a curse under his breath, knowing he had to get control. Regardless of the picture they would be painting for others, there was no going back. He would tell himself that a million times a day if he had to.

Kara entered the Racetrack Café. Unlike the last time she'd met Virgil for dinner and he'd taken her to a place they'd never dined in before, this was the very place they used to hang out most of the time. She was immediately flooded with memories of how they would meet here after work before heading to her place or his.

Instead of calling, he had texted her instructions to meet here. At first she'd found it odd he would choose this place since it had such a history for them. Then again, she figured if he wanted to make it seem as if they were getting back together, this was the perfect place.

The first thing she noticed was that the café wasn't crowded, which was unusual for a Thursday night.

She glanced around and saw him. When their gazes met, she suddenly felt a little breathless and forced her feet forward to where he was now standing. Unlike her, he'd taken the time to go home and change into jeans. Since she had a late business meeting, she was still wearing her two-piece suit and heels.

"Sorry, I'm late," she said, trying to ignore the rapid beating of her heart. "Late meeting."

"No problem," he said, sitting back down after she slid into the booth across from him. "Glad you could make it. I saw you when you parked so I went ahead and ordered your Arnold Palmer."

"Thanks." She tried not to smile at the thought that he remembered her favorite drink. "You said we needed to meet to plan a strategy." She could tell he'd showered because her nostrils picked up the clean scent of man as well as his familiar aftershave. It had always been her favorite.

"Yes, but that discussion can come later. I thought we'd eat first," he said, breaking into her thoughts.

Kara tried to avoid looking at him by

glancing around. "Not a lot of people here tonight."

"There's a big Panthers pep rally going on at the stadium. They're gearing up for tomorrow's preseason opener against the Eagles."

"Oh."

He chuckled. "You're still not a football fan, I see."

"No. Some things never change, I guess." Their gazes connected and she couldn't help but feel the chemistry. The same one they'd always shared. Despite how much he disliked her, that hadn't changed, which was a good thing.

He finally broke eye contact with her when the waitress delivered their drinks. She quickly took a sip of hers and appreciated the feel of the cold liquid moving down her throat. She felt hot and needed to cool off. Sitting across from her was the one man who had the ability to make her burn, both inside and out.

"So how was your day, Kara?"

She glanced back over at him. "Do you really want to know or are you just being nice?"

Virgil held her gaze. "Both." Bougard Enterprises was the only reason he was sitting across from her now and not at that pep rally like everyone else. But still the man in him appreciated a good-looking woman, which was why he'd felt a tightening in his gut when he'd seen her walk into the café. "So tell me, how was your day?"

He watched her shrug her shoulders before taking another sip of her drink. "It went rather well, actually. I was hired to do a series of leadership seminars at Lufton Financial Services. And I also found out that I've been nominated by our local league of women voters for Businesswoman of the Year."

A smile automatically touched his lips. He was genuinely happy for her. "Congratulations for both achievements."

"Thanks."

"We need to celebrate this weekend."

She lifted a brow. "We do?"

"Yes. It will be a good excuse for us to be seen together. I'll make the arrangements."

She reached out and the touch of her hands on his sent stirring sensations ricocheting all through him, sensations he was sure she felt, too. But she didn't let go. "No, let me make the arrangements, Virgil."

While gazing into her eyes, he thought like he always had that they were the most beautiful pair any woman could possess. Tonight he saw a determination in them that he hadn't seen in a long time, if ever.

"All right. You make all the arrangements," he said, giving in and not having a problem doing so. He liked the way her touch was making him feel, although he wished otherwise.

She smiled and released his hand, and damn if that smile didn't make his gut tighten even more. "You won't be disappointed," she said.

A short while later Kara pushed her plate aside. Virgil had invited her here to discuss strategies but so far they hadn't done that. Over dinner she'd asked questions about his family and when he'd told her his sister was pregnant, she couldn't help but smile.

She'd met Leigh and liked her a lot. Right before she and Virgil had broken up Leigh and Chad had gotten engaged. Kara had been surprised to get an invitation to the wedding but because she'd known Virgil would not have wanted her there, she hadn't attended. But she had sent a wedding gift. And now to hear that Leigh and Chad would be parents was wonderful news.

And when she'd asked, he'd told her about his father's family, some of whom she'd gotten to know when she had attended one of the Bougard family reunions with him in Houston. Matthew had come from a large family that consisted of seven brothers and three sisters. Of all his siblings Matthew had been the only one who hadn't attended college in Texas. Leaving home to attend Morehouse had been a big step and then settling down in Charlotte instead of returning to Houston after graduation had been another one. To compensate, he'd made certain both his son and daughter had been Texans by birth by making sure a pregnant Rhona had been in Houston when it was time for her to deliver.

Sitting here with him, chatting amiably, she couldn't help remembering the last time they'd dined together. She'd mentioned the possibility of them becoming friends and he'd flat out rejected the idea. She hoped he'd change his stance on that since they'd be seeing a lot of each other in the coming weeks. But she had to be realistic and remember Virgil was merely playing a role, one he intended to play to the hilt to benefit his company.

When their dishes had been cleared away, Virgil asked, "Have you noticed a couple of people looking over here at us?"

His question made her discreetly scan the café. It wasn't as empty as it had been, which meant the pep rally had ended. Virgil was right. Several people were openly staring at them, and Kara wondered if it had anything to do with the article appearing in this morning's newspaper. Thanks to *Flo on the Ro,* they were now the couple to watch.

"Give me your hands."

She looked back at Virgil. Not understanding his request, she complied anyway. He took her hands and entwined their fingers. She raised her brow while keeping her gaze trained on his face, trying to ignore the warmth of his fingers interwoven with hers. She was sure every cell in her body was heating up.

"Now we're giving them something to look at," he said in a deep husky voice that sent shivers down her spine.

"Are we?"

A smile touched the corners of his lips. "If you don't believe me just watch." And he then leaned and kissed their joined hands.

Kara couldn't stop the tremble that immediately coursed through her. She licked her lips when a familiar sensation stirred in the lower part of her body. "Do you think this is necessary?" she asked, letting out a slow, controlled breath.

"Don't you?" he asked softly. "Tell me what you think since you came up with the action plan. Was this not what you had in mind for the woman I was to date exclusively? Were we not supposed to give people the impression that we're all into each other?"

"Yes, but I wasn't supposed to be that woman, Virgil."

"But unfortunately, Kara, you are now that woman. Now lean toward me a bit. Don't ask why, just do it."

Drawing in a deep breath, and with their hands interlinked and heat spreading up her thighs, she leaned in closer. And that's when he leaned in and brushed his lips softly against hers. She figured the kiss was meant to be quick, however, instead of either of them leaning back, their lips remained mere inches from each other. The most logical thing was to kiss again. So they did. This one lasted longer than the last, and when he swept his tongue across her lips, she felt fire curling in her stomach.

When their lips parted he tilted his head and looked at her and said in a deep throaty voice, "I think that will do for now."

"Will it?" she asked in a breathless whisper.

"Yes," he said, slowly releasing her hands. "Now it's time to leave."

"But I thought we were here to plan our strategy."

A smile touched the corners of his lips. "We just did. Come on and let me walk you to your car."

CHAPTER 10

The next morning Virgil gazed out his bedroom window and thought back on last night at the café with Kara. For the umpteenth time he tried convincing himself that kissing her had served a purpose. They'd had an audience so it had been the perfect time to put on a show.

But did he have to kiss her a second time and taste her with his tongue?

There was no doubt in his mind that he had felt something in those kisses, something he hadn't counted on. It was not intended to mean anything. He'd been merely acting out a part and nothing else. However, the moment his mouth had touched hers, emotions he hadn't expected had flooded him. Those emotions should have been buried long ago, never to resurface again.

Some emotions were to be expected, he told himself. After all, regardless of the reason they'd broken up, Kara had been the one and only woman he'd ever loved. Not feeling something would have been impossible.

He had walked her to her car and, when he'd opened the door and she'd slid her body onto the leather seat, exposing a luscious thigh in the process, a pang of desire had shot through him. He'd been tempted to act on it so he'd given in to temptation and placed a kiss on the side of her throat. He'd gone even further and used his tongue to cop a taste when he licked her skin there.

Kara's sharp intake of breath had let him know she'd felt it. There had been no logical reason for his tongue to come into contact with her skin, and now he was paying for his actions. He was convinced the taste of her had somehow saturated his insides. After she'd driven off, he had quickly walked to his car, gotten inside and driven home totally aroused. He still was.

He didn't want to be sexually attracted to Kara. It had taken only a kiss to show that she could still get under his skin. And if that wasn't bad enough, the taste of her had him thinking of nothing else but tasting her again. And why on earth had he suggested they spend the weekend together? What had he been thinking?

The cell phone on his nightstand rang but he didn't have to answer it to know who was calling. It was Uriel. Uriel and his wife, Ellie, were spending the summer on Cavanaugh Lake, which was located a few miles from Gatlinburg.

Crossing the room, he picked up the phone. "Yes, U?"

"I came into town yesterday to attend the pep rally. Afterward a group of us went to the Racetrack Café and I heard you'd been there earlier with Kara. I also heard the two of you were all lovey-dovey." There was a brief pause before Uriel asked, "So, what's going on, V? Are you and Kara getting back together?"

"Not in a million years," Virgil replied in a gruff voice.

"In that case you have some explaining to do."

Virgil rolled his eyes. "Do I?"

"What do you think?"

Virgil drew in a deep breath. He didn't want his godbrothers getting the wrong idea about him and Kara. "Have you had breakfast yet?"

"No."

"Good. Join me, I'll explain everything."

"Okay. Where?"

"Meet me at the Racetrack Café in a half hour."

Kara stretched her body, not ready to get out of bed just yet. She glanced over at the clock and thought since she didn't have any appointments this morning there was no rush to get to the office. She would just lie here a minute longer and bask in her memories from yesterday.

He had kissed her. She would admit by Virgil Bougard's standards both kisses had been rather chaste. She knew from past experiences that Virgil had the ability to plow you with a kiss that could make your head swoon for days. But the lasting effect had been just as powerful. Then when he'd walked her to her car, he had licked her throat. The feel of his tongue on her skin had stirred something deep within her.

And then he'd suggested they spend some time together this weekend, to be seen in public as a couple. She would plan the activity and she already had an idea what she wanted them to do. They would —

Her cell phone rang, interrupting her thoughts and quickening her pulse. Virgil had her number. Was he calling her?

Reaching for the phone, she glanced at caller ID and felt her heart sink. It was

Marti. It had been months since the two of them had communicated and she couldn't help wondering what her sister wanted. She sat up in bed and clicked on the phone. "Yes, Marti?"

"Is the article I read in yesterday's newspaper true?" Marti asked excitedly. "Are you and Virgil really back together?"

Kara frowned. Why would Marti sound happy for them after all she'd done? "And what if we are?"

"Then I'm happy for you. I know you don't believe me but I truly am. I was wrong about Virgil, and in trying to protect you, I went too far. I know you hate me and —"

"I don't hate you but you had no right to do what you did and then to brag about it to the person you were talking to on the phone. You know the pain I went through when I thought Virgil was unfaithful. You let me go through that. You even had the gall to give me your shoulder to cry on when you deliberately lied about him."

"I thought I was protecting you, Kara. Why can't you believe that? Why can't you forgive and forget so we can move on?"

Kara drew in a deep breath. Hadn't she wondered the same thing about Virgil when he hadn't accepted her apology? But there was one difference. "Because I don't believe you regret what you did. Don't forget I overheard that conversation you had with that person on the phone. You were bragging and boasting about how you screwed up my relationship with Virgil. If I didn't know better, I'd think the reason you did it was because you wanted him for yourself."

"That's not true! I told you why I did it. I didn't believe he really loved you and thought he would eventually hurt you. You're my baby sister and I didn't want you to go through the pain that . . ."

When Marti didn't finish what she was about to say, Kara asked, "What? What were you going to say, Marti?"

"Nothing," Marti said, much too quickly to suit Kara. "I was wrong about him and I'm sorry. But it's not about us anymore, Kara. It's about Mom and Dad."

Kara frowned. "What are you talking about?"

"They're on bad terms because of us. It's all my fault that there's a rift between me and you, and I hate that Mom and Dad are involved. Please let's meet this morning for breakfast. We need to at least talk, Kara."

Kara didn't say anything for a minute. She hated how the disjunction between her and Marti was affecting her parents. Maybe she should take Virgil's lead and forgive but not forget. She doubted she could ever trust her sister again.

"I need to shower and get dressed. It will take an hour."

"Great!"

Kara tried not to notice the excitement in Marti's voice. "You decide where."

"You know I'm going to say Racetrack Café. Their waffles are to die for."

She shook her head. Unknowingly Marti had selected the place where she'd dined just last night with Virgil. How could she sit there this morning and not be swamped by memories of his kisses?

"So there you have it, U. The only reason I'm coming within ten feet of Kara is for business."

Uriel Lassiter lifted a brow. "You sure about that? From what I heard, your mouth was playing around hers pretty damn good."

Virgil frowned. "That kiss was just for show."

"Whatever you say," Uriel said in a tone suggesting he didn't believe him. "Did you finally come around to accepting Kara's apology?"

"I told her I would forgive her but I wouldn't forget."

"People make mistakes. Even you, V."

Virgil's frown deepened. "You're right. My biggest mistake was ever falling in love with her."

Uriel shook his head. "I'd be wasting my time if I told you to let it go. I've suggested it before and you haven't. You recall how for all those years I avoided Ellie."

Yes, Virgil remembered. Ellie had played a teenage prank on Uriel that had taken him nearly ten years to forget. Eventually he had and the two were now married.

"I told you that I accepted her apology."

"But you're still holding a grudge."

"I am not holding a grudge. Doing so would require too much time and effort, and I don't intend to give Kara any more of either than I have to."

Uriel took a sip of his coffee. "I'm surprised Kara agreed to go along with pretending to be in an exclusive affair with you."

Virgil shrugged. "She wasn't happy about it. But Kara is getting paid to improve my image, no matter what it takes for her to do so."

Uriel gave him a hard glare. "I hope you don't have any sort of revenge on your mind, V."

Virgil didn't say anything as he took a sip of his coffee. He would be lying if he said the thought hadn't crossed his mind. As far as he was concerned if Kara hadn't believed her sister's lie they would still be together now. Possibly even married with a kid or two. Her lack of trust in him had ruined everything, including his belief in love.

"V?"

He met Uriel's gaze. "No, but I don't intend to make things easy for her."

"So in other words, you intend to be difficult."

A wry smile touched Virgil's lips. "Maybe. Maybe not."

"Well, I hope you don't plan to be difficult today."

Virgil raised a brow. "Why?"

"Because Kara just walked in and Marti is with her."

Virgil held Uriel's gaze in a hard stare. Then he slid his chair back, stood and said in a deadly calm voice, "Then by all means, U, let's go say hello to the Goshay sisters."

When the waitress placed the menu in front of them, Kara knew before they shared a meal, there was something she needed to ask her sister. For some reason she thought there was more to it than what Marti had told her.

"Marti, I need to know the truth as to why

you lied about Virgil."

"Why are you bringing that up again, Kara? I told you I was sorry and why I did it. Why can't we move on? It's not like you and Virgil haven't worked things out and aren't back together."

Kara didn't say anything, knowing her sister would be the last person she told the true nature of her and Virgil's relationship. "Regardless of whether Virgil and I are back together, Marti, I feel there is more to it. Something you aren't telling me."

"You're wrong. I told you my reason so can we just drop it?"

She heard the annoyance in Marti's voice and wished she could drop it, but for some reason she couldn't. And another thing . . . She needed her sister to understand that rebuilding their relationship would take time. The only reason she was even here now was because of what Marti had shared about their parents.

Kara suddenly felt a rush of heat travel up her spine. When she glanced around she saw him. Virgil. And he, along with his god-brother Uriel, was headed straight toward their table. Virgil's features were unreadable so she had no idea of his mood. The one thing she did know was that Marti definitely wasn't one of his favorite people.

She inhaled sharply. Would Virgil confront Marti? The café was crowded and the last thing Virgil needed was make a scene. She could just imagine the article that would appear in *Flo on the Ro.* Virgil's image would go from bad to worse.

Knowing she had to take quick action, she stood, pasted a huge smile on her face and reached out to embrace Virgil when he reached her table. "Virgil, I didn't know you were having breakfast with Uriel here this morning," she said, wrapping her arms around him and looking up at him with a pleading look in her smile.

And then she leaned up on tiptoe and brushed her mouth against his in what was intended to be a quick kiss. When she was about to pull back, Virgil wrapped his arms around her and despite where they were, slanted his mouth across hers.

Virgil figured two could play whatever game Kara was playing for Marti's benefit. Although it irked him that they had her in their audience, at the moment he didn't give a damn since an opportunity was an opportunity, especially if it was for the media's sake. There was no reason he shouldn't take advantage, so he gave her a short, hot, tongue-stroking kiss.

It hadn't been the kiss he'd he wanted to

plow her mouth with, but for now it had been effective. When he released her, he said softly, "Good morning to you, sweetheart. Uriel called this morning and we decided to get together for breakfast."

With every degree of control Virgil had, he turned and looked at Marti, fighting hard to keep the glare out of his eyes and the sting from his voice. "Marti."

"Virgil."

And then Kara gave Uriel a hug. "Hi, Uriel."

Uriel smiled. "How are you, Kara?" He then looked over at Marti. "And you?"

"I'm fine, Uriel. Thanks for asking" was Marti's response.

With pleasantries, even fake ones, out of the way, Virgil took Kara's hand, lifted it to his lips and kissed it. "Made plans for our weekend yet?"

Kara nodded. Her body reeled when she felt his tongue swipe across her fingers. "I'm working on them," she said, trying to keep her voice normal as sensations swept through her mind. What he'd done had been deliberate. Just like when his tongue had swept across her neck last night. When they'd been a couple, he'd had a penchant for using his tongue to lick her all over.

He smiled at her. "Good. I'll call you later."

"You guys leaving already? You're free to join us," Marti invited.

Kara frowned. Did her sister really think Virgil would? Marti had to know the high degree of disdain he held her in.

Virgil looked down at Marti and said politely, "No thank you." He then turned his attention back to her. "Have a good day."

"You, too," she said, knowing his patience with Marti had probably worn thin by now. As a way to thank him for not losing his cool with her sister, she leaned up and brushed her lips against his cheek.

When Kara stepped back, she knew they'd given a good show to anyone watching . . . and it seemed a number of people were. "We'll definitely talk later," he said softly.

She deciphered the underlying message in his words. They would talk and she had a feeling it was a conversation she'd prefer not having with him.

Later that day Kara had finished a survey on a potential client when her cell phone rang. When she picked it up off her desk and saw it was Virgil, her breath caught in her throat. She had deliberately put off calling him, and Virgil, probably sensing as much, had decided to contact her instead.

She braced herself for the conversation they were about to have. "Yes, Virgil?"

"What are our plans for this weekend?"

Kara drew in a deep breath. She wondered if he remembered that was the question he would call and ask her every Friday when they were dating. During those days it was a foregone conclusion that their Saturdays and Sundays would be spent together. She wished she could go back in time and relive those days when the two of them had been so much in love and enjoyed being together.

"How does spending the day at Caro-winds sound?" she asked him.

Of all things, she hadn't expected the sound of his rich chuckle. She was so surprised by it that she held her phone away from her a minute just to stare at it, to make sure the sound had actually come from her phone. She fought off getting all emotional because she hadn't thought she would ever hear the sound of laughter in his voice again.

"Why aren't I surprised?" he asked with deep amusement in his voice.

"I don't know. Why aren't you?" Even if he wasn't surprised by what she'd planned, she definitely was surprised by how well he was taking it.

"Well, for one thing, I know how much

you enjoy amusement parks, particularly those scary rides."

His words made her smile. "You enjoy them as much as I do."

He chuckled again. "That is true."

She leaned back in her chair and recalled how they both had a thrill for the wild side, especially those crazy roller coasters that could send your heart racing and your mind spinning. For them, the scarier the better. Carowinds, a four-hundred-acre amusement park that boasted over fifteen such rides, had been one of their favorite places to visit on the weekends. They'd found those heart-stopping rides the perfect way to relieve stress.

Thinking she owed him a reason for her choice, she said, "I figured since it's local, we'll be seen and that would be good."

Virgil didn't say anything for a minute. Kara's words had reeled him back in and made him remember that the trip to Carowinds, like everything else they would be doing together, was to serve a purpose.

"You figured right. So what time do you want me to pick you up in the morning?"

"Um, what about ten?"

"That will work." There was no reason not to end their conversation so he said, "I'll see you then. Goodbye."

"Virgil, wait!"

"Yes?"

"About Marti . . ."

His jaw tightened. "What about her?"

He noticed the slight pause before she replied. "Thank you for handling things the way you did this morning, considering everything."

Tossing the pen on his desk, while trying not to recall the pen had been part of a set she'd given him for his birthday, he said, "Your sister is your problem, Kara, not mine. This morning wasn't the first time I've seen Marti since finding out about her part in our breakup."

"So you knew? Even before I told you six months ago?"

"Yes."

"But how? I never told you how I'd come across the information."

No, she hadn't told him, he thought, standing to stretch his tall frame. "You didn't have to tell me. I figured it out. I was never one of your sister's favorite people, although around you she pretended otherwise."

"I never knew."

He paused a minute before he continued. "Like I said, Kara, Marti is your problem. How you deal with your sister is your business. But just so you know, I can barely tolerate being around her. You might have apologized but she never has, which makes me believe she doesn't regret what she did."

"She says the reason she did it was because she thought you would eventually hurt me."

"I never gave her reason to think that, Kara. You and I had been happy together. For her to tell such a lie is unacceptable. Who would do what she did to their sister, no matter what they thought?"

Kara didn't answer his question and Virgil knew there was no logical way for her to do so anyway. "Look, I have a lot of work to do before I can leave here. I'll see you tomorrow morning, Kara."

"All right."

When he disconnected their call, he shoved his hands into the pockets of his pants and walked over to the window. Bringing up the past with Kara would serve no purpose. She had always looked up to her sister and thought she could do no wrong. It must have been hard on her to find out that had been a lie, as well. But then why should he care?

Glancing at his watch, he got back to work. He still had a lot to do before he could go home, and he wanted to get to bed early. He'd need a good night's sleep to be ready for Carowinds in the morning. And for a day with Kara.

CHAPTER 11

Virgil arrived at Kara's home at precisely ten o'clock on Saturday morning, punctual as usual. Glancing at herself in the mirror one final time, she was satisfied with the shorts set she'd purchased a few weeks ago and never worn. As she moved toward the door, she told herself it was just a coincidence it was purple, Virgil's favorite color on her.

The weather forecast indicated it would be a beautiful day with no chance of rain, perfect for the amusement park. But the closer she got to the door, the more nervous she felt. Truthfully it had nothing to do with the weather and everything to do with the man. She tried reminding herself this date was for business purposes only. Still, he was the man she had once loved, still loved, so being around him and keeping her emotions at bay wouldn't be easy. She had no other choice but to try.

When she opened the door, a bright ray of sunlight came through almost blinding her, but not before she got an eyeful of the man standing on her doorstep. He was wearing a pair of jeans that tapered down muscular thighs, and a Carolina Panthers T-shirt that covered broad shoulders and a masculine chest. She of all people knew how he liked spending time at the gym and she could definitely see it was time well spent. Every bit of Virgil Bougard looked sexy and could make any woman drool. Like she would be doing if she didn't get a grip.

She angled her head to look up at him. He had an unreadable expression on his face so she had no idea what kind of mood he was in. "Good morning, Virgil."

"Good morning. You ready?"

"Yes, I just have to lock up. You can come in."

"I'd rather not. I can stay right here until you're done," he said.

"Yes, but if anyone is watching they might find your actions odd."

Virgil knew what she'd said was true. If anyone was watching, he figured they would expect them to greet with a kiss. He had no problem carrying that out, so he leaned forward and brushed a kiss across her lips. At her surprised expression he said, "Just in case someone is looking." Then he walked past her to enter her home.

He came to a stop in her foyer and, since her home was an open concept plan, from where he stood he could see her huge living room, dining area and large eat-in kitchen. All the rooms had high ceilings, and wall-to-wall windows provided a brightness he'd always loved.

He wished he didn't remember all the times he'd spent here with her. How many times they'd shared wine and kisses while sitting at her breakfast bar or made love on her sofa or in front of her fireplace. Or how many times he'd stood here, in the same spot, just seconds before sweeping her up in his arms to carry her to the bedroom.

"I won't be but a minute," she said, moving past him.

When she walked by, he couldn't help drawing her scent into his nostrils. She smelled good. She looked good, as well. He couldn't stop his gaze from roaming across her backside as she headed for the kitchen. She still had the best-looking ass of any woman he knew. And her legs — long and gorgeous — looked good in shorts.

When she'd opened the door, one of the first things he'd noticed was that she was wearing purple. She had to remember how much he enjoyed seeing her in that color. To him, it did something to her silver-gray eyes. It also did something to his libido like it was doing now.

"I'm all set."

While he'd been buried in his thoughts, she had returned and was standing in front of him. Too damn close as far as he was concerned. For the past few days, he'd played around with her mouth, brushing his lips across it, and even getting a lick or two on occasion. But what he really wanted to do was pull her into his arms and kiss her like they used to kiss. It would be the kind of kiss that would make her purr and make him moan deep in his throat.

The kind of kiss he needed right now but was fighting like hell to do without.

"Virgil?"

He'd gotten lost in his thoughts again. "Yes?"

"I said I'm ready to go."

He drew in a deep breath. "Okay, let's not keep all those rides waiting."

Kara would be the first to admit it was a fun day. It was as if she and Virgil had put the reason they were spending time together to the back of their minds. Like kids, they were excited to try a new ride, one scarier than all the others. It didn't matter that the lines had been long; they agreed the wait had been well worth it.

With the thrill of the rides also came complications. Packed tight into the compartment together, she tried not to notice how his thigh would rub against hers or how, on a few of the rides, she had to practically sit in his lap. And then there were the times he wrapped his arms around her, to make sure she was okay during the rides when she would scream her lungs out. At one point she recalled gripping his thigh when one of the rides seemed to nearly topple them over.

More than once she had glanced over at him to see him staring at her and wondered what he'd been thinking about. During one of those times their gazes had held and then he had leaned down and brushed his lips against hers. There hadn't been a reason for him to do so, but she had let him, a part of her even wishing it could have lasted longer.

At the end of each ride it seemed the sexual chemistry between them skyrocketed. She wasn't sure if it was because of the thrill left over from the rides or the sensuous energy they seemed to generate whenever they were together. And as if it was the most natural thing to do, they began walking around the amusement park holding hands.

They had just ridden their last ride of the day and were headed to the parking lot, and they were still holding hands. He only let go of her to help her into the car. A new car, she noted, since it still had that new car smell.

"Hungry?" he asked when he was seated beside her.

She couldn't help but grin. "I shouldn't be after all that junk food I ate. I hadn't realized just how much I missed eating a Carowinds hot dog." She paused a minute. "Thanks for bringing me here today, Virgil."

He chuckled. "Need I remind you it was your choice?"

She smiled. "No, but you didn't have to do it. In fact you really didn't have to suggest that we do anything this weekend."

Kara was right, Virgil thought, he didn't have to. So why had he? He had convinced himself if they broke the ice with this weekend then spending time with her next weekend around his parents wouldn't be so awkward. Because he didn't want to explore any other reasons, he changed the subject. "How are things going at work?"

"Do you really want to know?"

When he stopped the car at a traffic light,

he glanced over at her. "I always supported you and your work, Kara," he said.

She nodded. "Yes, you did. And I appreciated it."

When the traffic light changed, he resumed driving. It was on the tip of his tongue to say he didn't want her appreciation. He wanted her. There, he'd admitted it to himself because deep down he knew that he did. At some point his anger toward her had transformed into lust for her. When it came to Kara, over the years he had learned how to deal with his anger, but he wasn't sure how to handle this high degree of lust. Being around her today had reminded him of how things used to be. And in trying to put his animosity behind him and move on, he'd somehow rekindled his physical need for her. And it had gotten restored to a level he wasn't sure he could handle.

What he should do here and now was tell her that hiring her had been a mistake and there was no way they could continue to work together even if it meant improving his image. His father would just have to deal with that decision. But to be honest, he doubted that even he could deal with that decision. Mainly because just hanging around Kara for the past few days had accomplished the one thing he hadn't wanted to have happen. It had overwhelmed not only his common sense but also his self-control. If he licked her one more time he was liable to detonate.

"Virgil?"

He glanced over at her. "Yes?"

"If you're hungry, instead of stopping somewhere, I could make a pot of chili."

Now she wasn't playing fair. No matter what time of year it was — fall, winter, spring or summer — he loved her chili. His grandmother in Houston had shared the family recipe with her when Kara had gone with him to one of his family reunions. He didn't know how she'd done it, but hers was just as good as the chili Hattie Lee Bougard was known to make.

"I would hate for you to go to the trouble," he said, while inwardly hoping she didn't mind. He hadn't been to Houston in a year and missed his grandmother's home-cooked meals. His mother could cook, but when she'd gone back to college to get her master's and then her PhD, his father had taken over cooking duties. Although the meals had been all right, they hadn't been anything like his mom's. And now his parents enjoyed dining out, so there was no hope of ever getting invited over for dinner.

"No problem at all," she said. "In fact I've got all the ingredients I need. Won't take but a minute to prepare it."

When he came to another traffic light he glanced over at her. "You sure?"

"Positive."

He continued looking at her. When he held her gaze a little longer than he knew he should have, he broke eye contact but figured it had been too late. In that space of time, something intensely sexual had passed between them. He was certain that she was aware of it as much as he was. In the year they'd dated, he'd discovered that Kara was a very passionate woman. On top of that, she was as sensual as she was passionate.

And he was well aware that Kara knew just how much he enjoyed sex. More specifically, sex with her. Eventually he had stopped thinking about it as just sex and that's when he'd known he had fallen in love with her. But those days were over and anything they did now would be nothing more to him than sex. And he didn't even want that with her. Engaging in any kind of physical relationship with her was too risky for his peace of mind.

He quickly glanced back over at her and wished he could focus on something else. Why did he find her so captivating? So

156

damn appealing? He wished like hell he didn't remember how good she looked naked. Drawing in a deep breath, he forced his gaze back on the road. He decided to get on the interstate to avoid the traffic lights so he wouldn't be tempted to seek her out.

A short while later she said his name. "Virgil?"

He glanced over at her. "Yes?"

"You okay?"

He drew his brows together. "Why wouldn't I be?"

"You just passed my exit."

He glanced at the interstate markers and saw that he had. "Sorry about that. My mind was occupied. I'll turn around at the next exit."

Virgil knew that he needed to concentrate on what he was doing and where he was going and not the woman sitting beside him. It was easier said than done.

Kara didn't have to wonder where Virgil's mind had been. She knew him and knew the look she saw in his eyes each and every time he had looked at her today. He wanted her. That was obvious, just like it was probably as obvious that she wanted him. But she knew him well enough to know he would fight the desire for her tooth and nail. In his mind he didn't love her anymore, which meant that he didn't want to share any kind of relationship with her ever again, sexual or otherwise. It was too bad his body wasn't getting the message.

During the year they'd dated she'd learned a lot about men in general and about Virgil specifically. When he loved he loved hard. When he hated he hated just as hard. Over the past four years she figured he had convinced himself he detested her with every bone in his body. Yet over the past few days he was beginning to discover that although the love might be dead, the lust was not only alive and well but had taken on a life of its own. And she figured that was the crux of his problem. It was a problem that he would have to figure out how to deal with on his own.

Kara had figured out hers. She still loved him and would always love him. It would be up to him to decide whether he was dead set against letting her have a place in his life and heart again. She was determined not to make that decision easy for him — this bachelor who was so unforgiving.

He had exited the interstate and was easing his car to a stop at a traffic light. She kept her gaze focused ahead, knowing as soon as he brought the car to a stop he would be looking over at her. Let him look, she thought. Hopefully he liked what he saw.

She could feel the heat of his gaze move up and down her body, lingering on her bare legs before slowly moving up past her hips and waist toward her breasts. He wasn't blind, so she was certain he was fully aware that her nipples had hardened and were pressing against her shirt. It was her guess he was thinking of just what he would like to do with those nipples. Oh, how she used to love the feel of him sucking on them.

She had timed it perfectly to when his scanning eyes would move upward from her body to reach her face. That's when she turned her head and their gazes met. She felt a stirring in the pit of her stomach when she read desire in the depths of his eyes. The penetrating stare was having a hypnotic effect on her, and unlike him, she wasn't trying to fight it. In fact, she was embracing it, just like she intended to embrace him when and if he ever made a move.

The driver of the car behind them blasted his horn, letting them know the light had changed and they were holding up traffic.

Without saying anything Virgil broke eye contact with Kara to concentrate on his driving again. He found it hard to believe

159

time hadn't eradicated the urgency he was feeling for her, a sexual hunger so deep he could feel it in his bones. Even more so in his groin. Evidently, even after all this time, she was either not out of his system like he'd thought or she'd miraculously managed to wiggle her way back in. His mind went into a tailspin because that was the last thing he wanted to happen.

Virgil knew at that moment that agreeing to have dinner with her was not a good idea. Chili wasn't the only thing he would want once he was inside her home.

"I've changed my mind about dinner," he said. "As much as I would love to eat some of your chili, I just remembered something I need to do."

"Okay, I understand. Perhaps some other time."

Not if he could help it, he thought. He would make sure when their paths crossed again that he had his head screwed on right. Being overwhelmed by lust was the last thing he wanted or needed.

The rest of the drive to her house was done in silence and he couldn't help wondering what she was thinking. No conversation was taking place between them, and the quiet caused every primitive male instinct he possessed to be on full alert. He was aware when she shifted her body, making her skin slide against the leather seat, and when she stretched out one of her legs to a more comfortable position. When he slowed down for traffic, he glanced over at her. She was looking straight ahead out the windshield and he thought her profile was simply beautiful.

It was his opinion that no woman should look this good after going on over a dozen or so crazy rides. She should look sweaty, ruffled and exhausted, not cool, refreshed and relaxed. His gaze lowered to her hands, which were resting in her lap. He wished he didn't remember those hands and what they could do when they touched him all over, especially in certain places. Those hands had the ability to stroke him to dizzying heights. Make him moan. Render him hard just thinking about it.

He shifted his gaze from her hands to her lips, recalling how on several occasions her lips and hands worked together to drive him as wild as those rides had done today. Even wilder.

The car horn that blasted behind him was a reminder that, once again, he was paying too much attention to her. He refocused on the road and moved the car forward, feeling a tightness in his crotch. Hell, his desire for her wasn't going away. It was getting worse.

When he turned onto her street, she said, "Thanks for today, Virgil. I enjoyed myself." And when he pulled into her driveway, she added, "And you don't have to walk me to the door."

She was wrong. Yes, he had to walk her to her door. And it had nothing to do with any playacting but everything to do with the fire burning inside him. His control had abandoned him, taken a leap and at this point he couldn't get a grip even if he wanted to do so. He should be putting distance between them but he was too aware of the sexual need building with force inside of him. A need that just wouldn't go away. He knew his limits when it came to Kara and today they were being tested.

He brought the car to a stop and she proceeded to unbuckle her seat belt and he did the same. Intense heat had spiked in the area below his waist and was quickly spreading through other parts of him.

She glanced over at him with a questioning look after seeing he had removed his seat belt. "Really, Virgil, you don't have to walk me to the door. I'm okay."

She might be okay but he wasn't. "Yes, I do have to walk you to the door, Kara."

Evidently something in his tone told her

he was serious. She merely nodded before opening the car door, not waiting for him to do it for her. But she did pause and wait for him before she got out of the car.

When he reached her, she studied his face a second before extending her hand to him. Without hesitating, Virgil took it and then they moved toward her front door.

Kara knew he was determined to put distance between them, which was the reason he had changed his mind about staying for chili. But she couldn't help but be reminded of other times she and Virgil would return from a date and stroll up the walkway holding hands. During those times there had been no doubt in her mind that he wouldn't stop at her door, but that he'd follow her inside and then take her into his arms the moment the door closed behind them. She suddenly got weak in the knees remembering the intensity of the passion they would share, right there in her foyer. His kisses didn't just leave her breathless, they left her wanting more and more and more.

Upon reaching her door, she opened her cross-body purse, the very one he had given to her when they'd dated. It had been for no special occasion, he'd said when he'd done so. The card that he'd given her with the purse simply said, *I am so grateful that you're mine.*

When she took out the key, his finger reached out to trace along the intricate design of her purse. If he hadn't noticed the purse before, he was definitely noticing it now. Was he remembering that he was the one who'd given it to her? Did he remember what he'd written on the card, as well?

She turned to him before inserting the key in the lock. "Thanks again for a wonderful day, Virgil."

His dark, penetrating eyes stared down at her. "Aren't you going to invite me in, Kara?" he asked in a deep husky voice, one that sent sensual chills all over her body.

"I thought there was something you had to do."

"There is."

She frowned, finding what he said confusing. But instead of asking him to elaborate, she opened the door and he followed her inside.

"This is far enough," Virgil said when they stood in the foyer.

She turned to him questioningly. "For what?"

"This."

His mouth came down on hers, needing

what he'd only gotten swipes of the past few days. The quick tastes of her had been silky and warm, but now he wanted the intensity of the real thing. A tongue swipe across her lips just wouldn't do anymore. He needed to take the plunge. So he did.

Tipping her head back with the palm of his hand, he claimed her mouth as his tongue boldly swept inside, reacquainting itself with the special brand of intimacy they'd always shared. A deep sexual hunger, the same one that had been gnawing at his insides most of the day, stirred to life in his midsection. As if he'd opened some kind of erotic box, all the memories of their kisses came flooding back, arousing him in ways he wasn't used to.

Virgil wasn't sure if it was because of the length of time since he'd shared a kiss of this magnitude with her. Whatever the reason, jolts of sexual energy were rocking him to the bone, causing his tongue to dominate hers. The kiss was making him ravenous for her taste.

He was devouring her, and at this point, slowing down didn't seem to be an available option. And when he heard her moan, the sound compelled him to deepen the kiss even more. Swirling his tongue inside of her mouth, his mated with hers while coiling arousal settled deep in his core. He'd always enjoyed using his tongue to do all kinds of naughty things to her. They were things he'd been dreaming about doing since the day she had walked into that conference room to meet with him and his father.

He knew he needed to reel in his senses and pull back, but kissing her had always been his downfall. He'd never been able to get enough of her taste. It appeared that nothing had changed. He growled deep in his throat when fire seemed to spread through his veins.

Wrapping his arms around her waist, he urged her body closer to the hard fit of him. His hands moved from around her waist and shifted lower to cup her backside. Touching her this way felt good. And it reminded him that he'd always enjoyed touching her here on her bottom every chance he got.

Then there was the feel of her breasts pressing against his chest. The swollen buds were hard, causing his entire body to sizzle. He would love to strip her naked right here and taste her all over. Feed the flames of the heat he was feeling.

Kara had missed this. She had missed him. His tongue had taken control of her mouth while his hands were making all kinds of erotic designs on her backside. She needed this. She wanted this. It had been years since she'd felt passion like this. Four years, to be exact. Every part of her body was like a live wire sending all kinds of electrical currents through her.

He'd always been a master kisser and that hadn't changed. His lips were stroking her mouth in a way that had her reaching up, gripping his shoulders with her determination to match his kiss with the same hunger and intensity. She felt blood rush fast and furious through her veins and could feel her panties getting wet. Like always, their mouths fit together perfectly, while his tongue continued to explore every crevice of her mouth, using strokes so sensual, her stomach began spinning at the same time as her senses reeled.

She could taste the hunger in his kiss, the passion and desire. And when he plunged his tongue even farther into her mouth, sensations she could no longer contain began smoldering out of control and effectively blocking every single thought from her mind.

Suddenly he snatched his mouth from hers. Drawing in a long and deep breath, he stared down at her, holding her gaze but not saying anything. She could imagine what he was seeing. Half-lidded, liquid eyes. Flushed cheeks. A pair of well-kissed lips. When neither of them said anything, she was tempted to lean up and kiss him again. But his next words stopped her cold.

"This should not have happened." Removing his hands from around her, he took a step back. "Kissing this way could lead to things we don't want, Kara."

It was on the tip of her tongue to say *speak for yourself* because he had no idea what she wanted. But evidently he knew what he wanted and it wasn't her.

"You're right and I suggest you leave," she said, trying to keep the anger and hurt from her voice.

Obviously he heard it anyway and he reached out to grab hold of her hand. She pulled it back. "Don't, Virgil. You're right. Why should you waste good kisses on a woman you'll never love again? A woman you can barely tolerate being around? I get it. Thank you for looking out for my best interests."

Reaching behind him, she opened the door. "Goodbye, Virgil."

He stared at her a minute before saying, "I'll be leaving town this week for Orlando to meet with investors there. I get back the day before we're to attend that UNCC commencement ceremony together. I'll call you."

Tilting her head she pasted a smile on her face. "Have a safe trip."

He nodded, hesitating for only a second before walking out the door.

Chapter 12

Virgil gazed out of his hotel-room window to scan the grounds of one of Disney World's most prestigious resorts. It had been years since he'd visited Orlando, yet he could easily recall the times his parents had brought him and Leigh here as kids. Those had been fun days. And more than once when they'd been together, he'd thought of bringing Kara here.

Kara.

Drawing in a deep breath, he couldn't stop remembering this past weekend. Somehow he'd been able to let go of his bitterness and enjoy the day with her. It had been fun . . . until his desire for her had begun overruling his mind and taking hold of his body. He had immediately recognized the tormenting heat for what it was. And considering everything, the intensity of his attraction to her annoyed as well as mystified him.

Leave it to him to make matters even

worse when he'd taken her home. Why had he walked her to the door and then suggested she let him inside? The torture of wanting her had gotten so great that he'd given in to intense desire and kissed her. And he'd kissed her the way he'd been longing to for days. Even though her presence back in his life was temporary and strictly for business, his libido didn't seem to care.

Nor did his mouth give a damn since the taste of her still lingered there, even after five days. She'd always had the sweetest mouth but it seemed that over the years it had gotten sweeter and so satisfyingly delicious.

Leaving his place by the window, he moved to sit down at the desk in the hotel room, deciding he needed to get some work done. Already he'd held a number of meetings with potential investors. The International Investors Summit had a tendency to draw hedge fund corporations from all over the world. For that reason, it was always a good policy to have appointments scheduled way in advance, like he'd done. He'd gotten positive feedback from the six investors he'd met with so far.

His thoughts shifted back to Kara and that kiss he couldn't stop thinking about. And tasting. He leaned back in his chair and recalled the outfit she'd been wearing Saturday. It had been purple, his favorite color. Strolling around the amusement park, he'd noticed more than one man checking her out. She had legs that made any man want to take a second look and several had. More than once a streak of jealousy had raced through him. Why had he felt such possessiveness for a woman who wasn't his?

He had forgotten how tight the compartments were for the rides, and more than once their bodies had been crammed together, which had kicked his testosterone into full gear. Then his horny mind had looked forward to the times he'd been squeezed against her backside or when their thighs had been all but plastered against each other.

Virgil figured that had to be the reason he'd gone crazy once he'd gotten hold of her mouth. He had kissed her like hers was destined to be the last mouth he'd ever taste. And she had kissed him back, meeting him greed for greed.

And then somehow through all that ravenous pleasure, he'd found his senses and pulled back. Surprising himself as much as he'd probably surprised her. There had been no logical reason for him and Kara to stand in the middle of her foyer and go at each other's mouths like they'd been doing. No logical reason whatsoever.

That didn't stop his body from yearning for her every day since. Or stop his mouth from feeling like it was missing something vital. Or stop his erection from swelling each and every time he thought about her.

Like now.

And although he hated admitting it, he would give anything to have another such opportunity to take her into his arms and kiss her. Unfortunately, he was finding out the hard way that when it came to Kara, out of sight and out of mind didn't seem to work.

What he needed to do was what any successful businessman would do — come up with a game plan, some strategic move to eliminate the problem without alienating the source. He could tell before he'd left her place on Saturday that she hadn't appreciated what he'd said about kissing her being a mistake. Had she considered that a blatant rejection of her? And why should it bother him if she had?

He knew the answer without thinking about it. It bothered him because it was far from the truth. As much as he wanted to continue to convince himself he was completely and totally over Kara, there was still this sexual connection between them. At times it was so strong it cloaked them in an air of intimacy so thick he felt as if he was smothered by it.

So the question of the hour was this: just what exactly was he going to do about it? Since seeing her was basically part of *her* plan — the one she'd put together to improve his image — he needed to come up with a plan of his own. One designed to save his sanity.

Kara looked at herself in the full-length mirror and smiled, pleased with what she saw. She didn't think twice about why she had put so much time and effort into her appearance. If Virgil thought he could continue to resist her, then let him try. She would do everything in her power to make sure he didn't succeed.

After spending time with him on Saturday and after that kiss he'd given her when he brought her home, she was convinced he wasn't as immune to her as he claimed. Granted, initially she had been slightly peeved at how he'd abruptly ended their kiss and left her home last weekend, but her annoyance had dissipated when she realized what had happened. He had been running scared.

Virgil had enjoyed the kiss; she was sure of it. But something had made him pull back and break off the kiss, then go even further by saying crazy stuff like kissing her had been a mistake and wasn't anything either of them wanted. He had tried replacing desire with logic. A person could do that only so many times, and she was determined to make sure the clock ran out on him. Her goal was to make sure he took off the blinders and realized they deserved another chance to get it right.

She turned slightly in the mirror and smiled again. The sophisticated-looking purple dress was one she'd purchased this week when she'd gone shopping. At first she'd thought that wearing his favorite color again might be a bit too much. However she decided, just in case he hadn't realized her intent on Saturday, that today should leave no doubt in his mind what she was about.

Pleased by that very thought, she tossed her head, sending her shoulder-length hair swinging around her face. When she looked at herself again in the mirror she didn't miss the seductive gleam in her eyes. Granted, she would behave herself around his parents, but later, when she got him alone, she would make it her business to find out just how scared he could run.

She hadn't heard anything from him all week while he'd been in Orlando, but last evening she had gotten his text message advising her he would pick her up at nine this morning. A second text had followed a few hours later, indicating his parents had invited them to join them for brunch at Hammer's, a popular restaurant in town, following the commencement ceremony.

Kara had texted him back to say she had no problem doing that and that she thought it was a great strategic idea that the four of them be seen together that way. He hadn't responded and, if her guess was right, he might not have liked being reminded of their business arrangement. Oh, well.

The doorbell sounded. Quickly moving from her bedroom, she grabbed her purse and jacket as she headed for the door. It was time to put Operation Virgil Bougard in full swing.

"Welcome back, Virgil," Kara said, smiling before placing a quick kiss on his lips. "I'm ready." She then closed the door and strolled past him, moving briskly down the walkway.

Virgil almost stopped breathing for the thickness of the air settling in his lungs.

Dammit, where was the fire? Why was she moving so fast? He quickly reached out and grabbed her hand. "Whoa. What's going on?"

She glanced back at him. "What do you mean what's going on?"

"Usually when I pick you up there's a last-minute item you've got to grab and I have to wait inside a minute or two," he said. Come to think of it, that's how it worked with most women, he thought.

"Not this time. I've got everything and I'm ready. No need for you to have to wait on me for anything."

"Oh," he said, releasing her hand to walk beside her toward the car. He tried not to check out her dress. She was wearing purple again and he liked it. But it wasn't the color of the dress that had grabbed his total awareness of her this morning. It was the style. On anyone else it probably would look okay, but on her it elicited some thoughtful cravings. Not only that, a hot rush of desire was sending shivers through his body.

It wasn't that the dress was too over-the-top for the event they would be attending because it wasn't. In fact it was perfect for the occasion. But did it have to emphasize the svelte lines of her curves and the gracefulness of her long, gorgeous legs? And did it have to show off her small waist and generous breasts? The effect was so mind-blowing that he felt it all the way to his groin.

"Is there a problem?"

A frown marred his brow. "No, there's no problem," he said, opening the car door for her.

A spike of heat exploded in his gut when the dress flashed a portion of her thigh as she slid down into the car seat. Seeing her naked flesh could arouse him in a way nothing else could. And speaking of arousal . . . she could pretend nonchalance all she wanted, but he hadn't missed that crackle of sensual energy that flowed between them when they'd walked beside each other. And he was certain she felt it, as well.

"You can close the car door now."

He'd been caught staring. Trying to keep his features neutral, he closed the door and walked around to the other side of the car. After getting in and buckling his seat belt, he glanced over at her. "You look nice."

"Thanks."

"And your dress is purple."

She looked over at him, tilted her head back a little as if she needed to study his face. "I know what color my dress is, Virgil."

He stared at her, unable to figure out if she meant anything by that. Grabbing his sunglasses off the dash, he said, "Mom is looking forward to your joining us today."

"She knows the truth, right?"

"Yes, she knows the truth."

"Good."

As he backed the car out of her driveway, Virgil wasn't sure if it was a good thing or not.

"Rhona's speech was simply wonderful," Kara said to the two men at her side.

"Yes, it was," Matthew agreed. "She did an outstanding job, but then she always does," he added proudly.

Kara had always admired Virgil's parents' close relationship. It was obvious from the huge smile on Matthew's face that he was very proud of his wife. And, although she was certain Virgil was equally as proud, he hadn't said anything. In fact he hadn't said much to her since leaving her place. He had taken her hand as they had found their seats beside his father. The entire time her hand had been encased in his, she felt flutters that stirred deep in the pit of her stomach. When they sat down and he released her hand, the stirrings continued for a while. More than once she had glanced over at him to find him staring at her, making her wonder if he'd had a similar reaction.

It was hard not to stare back at him. He exuded that Virgil Bougard level of charismatic and sexual power. He looked good in his charcoal-gray suit. Blatantly sexy would be one way to describe him but not the only way. There was this indescribable masculine aura surrounding him and Kara was certain she wasn't the only female who noticed it. More than once she'd observed several others looking his way.

"There's my queen," Matthew said in a joyous tone, interrupting Kara's thoughts when Rhona could finally be seen among the throng of graduates and their families. Kara had always thought Rhona was a beautiful woman, one who didn't look a day over forty. Her honey-brown complexion was flawless, not a wrinkle in sight. And Kara knew Rhona credited her young features and slender form to a healthy diet and regular exercise.

"Come on, let's go meet her," Matthew said, leading the way.

Virgil surprised Kara when he captured her hand in his again. It took everything she had to ignore the spike of hot sensuality that raced up her spine. There were a lot of media in attendance, so she knew they had to play their roles convincingly.

When they met up with Rhona, Kara wasn't sure what to expect. She and Virgil's mother had run into each other several times over the past four years, either while out shopping or attending various social functions. The Bougards had always been kind to her whenever their paths had crossed. So kind that for a long while she'd wondered if Virgil had told them why they'd broken up.

After accepting a kiss from her husband, Rhona then turned smiling eyes toward Kara, reached out and gave her a hug. "Kara, it's good seeing you. Glad you could join us today."

Kara returned the smile. "I'm glad, as well."

Rhona then turned to her son. She placed a kiss on his cheek. "Thanks for coming, Virgil."

He smiled down at her. "There's no way I was going to miss it. You did us proud as usual, Mom."

"Thanks." She then glanced back and forth between Kara and Virgil before leaning over and whispering, "Playacting or not, the two of you look good together."

Before either of them could say anything — Kara wasn't sure what she would have said anyway — Matthew spoke up. "We might as well beat the crowd and head over to Hammer's."

"I agree," Virgil said, taking Kara's hand once again. And when he did, he felt it. That tingling sensation whenever he touched her. He was sure she felt it, too, which was why she glanced up at him. Their gazes connected and held until she broke eye contact when his father spoke.

"We're parked on the other side," Matthew said. "We'll see you guys at the restaurant."

"Okay." Virgil glanced around. Just as he'd figured, eyes were on them. More than a dozen people he didn't know had approached him and Kara, unashamedly confessing they were ardent readers of Flo's column and basically giving them the same compliment that his mother had given about how good they looked together.

"Don't forget about next Saturday, Virgil," Kara said as they walked to where his car was parked.

He looked down at her. "What about next Saturday?"

"The back-to-school drive. Your company is one of the major sponsors and is giving away over three hundred book bags. You agreed to be there to help give them out."

He nodded, remembering. "Will you be there?"

"There's no reason why I should. Your company has been doing it for years but this will be the first time you've made an appearance."

She was right. It would be. His father had always participated in such community events and more times than not, his mother had been there, as well. His parents had made a great team and always worked well together for the benefit of Bougard Enterprises.

He glanced at the woman walking beside him. He was still holding her hand, and for the time being, he had no inclination to release it.

CHAPTER 13

"I had a nice time with your parents, Virgil," Kara said the moment he brought his car to a stop in her driveway.

He turned toward her. "And I'm sure they had an equally nice time with you since they've always liked you."

He sounded a little annoyed by that, Kara thought. "I take it you think that's a bad thing."

He shrugged. "Doesn't matter one way or the other to me. Since you were the first woman I ever brought home for them to meet, it would make sense for you to have made a lasting impression."

She decided not to remind him that, according to his mother at dinner, she had been the *only* woman he'd ever brought home for them to meet. She could tell from the expression that had crossed Virgil's face that he hadn't particularly appreciated Rhona's mentioning that to her.

"I agree, it doesn't matter," she said. *What does matter, Virgil Bougard, is that you pretty much haven't taken your eyes off me all day.*

"Again, thanks for a nice day and you don't have to walk me to the door."

Her front porch was bathed in moonlight and she could clearly see his frown by the light shining into the car. "I wish you wouldn't do that," he said gruffly.

"Do what?" she asked, unbuckling her seat belt.

"Tell me what I don't have to do. I intend to walk you to your door, Kara."

"Okay. I was just trying to save you the bother."

When she reached to open her car door, he said, "And I'll get your door."

She pulled her hand back. "All right."

He unbuckled his seat belt, got out of the car and walked around the front of it to the passenger side. Sexiness was oozing from every part of his body — it was in his walk as well as his clothes. Earlier he had removed his suit jacket and she enjoyed looking at his broad shoulders and tight muscular chest outlined in his fitted dress shirt. Kara would admit that she'd kept a close eye on him today, just as he'd been doing with her.

He opened her car door and extended his

hand out to her. She took it and immediately sucked in a deep breath when a hot, raw and sensual spark of energy passed between them. That had been happening a lot today, especially when their hands touched.

Because he didn't step back, her body was nearly plastered to his when she got out of the car. Desire quickly soaked into her skin in a heated rush and she didn't have to be told what he was doing was deliberate. If his intent was a plan of seduction, she was one up on him. She had a plan of her own.

"You're blocking my way, Virgil."

He held her gaze. "Am I?"

"Yes."

"Sorry." He took a step back and then strolled beside her to the front door.

When they reached their destination, she turned to him. "Well, this is where we say goodbye. It was a longer day than either of us anticipated."

She was certain neither of them expected his parents to suggest at dinner they go back to their place for dessert since Rhona had baked her famous chocolate cake the day before. They had sat around laughing and talking while eating dessert, and the next thing she knew they were watching several movies on Matthew's new ninety-inch flat-screen television. Although the additional time spent with Virgil's parents had been unexpected, she had definitely enjoyed herself.

"You're not going to invite me in?"

"Why, do you want to come in?" *Like I don't know.*

His gaze slid down her body before moving back up to her face. His eyes met hers. "What if I told you I think we need to talk?"

From the look in his eyes, she knew talking was the last thing on his mind. She recognized that I-want-some-of-you look in his eyes. "Talk about what?"

"How to proceed in our relationship."

What relationship? They had a relationship? If they did it was news to her. "We don't have a relationship, Virgil. We have a business arrangement. You've made that pretty clear more than once."

"And that's what I need to talk to you about."

She gazed at him thoughtfully for a minute and then said, "Fine, we'll talk but only because you have me curious." She then took the key from her purse.

When she found it, he took it from her hand. And the moment their fingers touched, a jolt of sexual desire rocked her to the bone. She glanced up at him and a tight smile touched the corners of his lips.

"I felt it, too," he said, his eyes flaring with the same intense desire that she felt. "I've been feeling it all day and that's why we need to talk."

If he thought talking would solve their problem, then he was not thinking realistically. But instead of saying anything, she nodded.

He unlocked the door and then stood aside for her to enter.

Virgil followed Kara inside, and the moment he stepped into the foyer, he couldn't help remembering what had happened the last time he was here. He had given Kara a kiss in a way that should be outlawed. And nothing would satisfy him more than to do it again. But like he'd told her, they needed to talk. While in Orlando he'd come up with a plan, one he hoped she would go along with.

"Would you like something to drink?" she asked him.

He reined his thoughts in and noticed she had paused to remove the high heels from her feet. "That would be nice."

"You know where the refrigerator is. Help yourself. I need to grab my flats."

He watched her walk off toward her

bedroom and his gaze was fixed on her backside with every step she took. She damn sure looked good in that purple dress. He hadn't been able to keep his eyes off her most of the day. And he'd wanted to touch her every chance he got, which was why he'd taken hold of her hand a lot. Spending time at his parents' place had reminded him of other times they'd joined the folks for movie night. When she went into her bedroom and closed the door behind her, he rubbed a hand down his face and quickly walked to the kitchen. He definitely needed a drink.

Moving through her living room, he glanced around and noticed a number of changes she'd made. Several new pieces of furniture, more artwork on her walls. When he stepped into the kitchen, he immediately noticed new stainless-steel appliances. She had talked about getting rid of her old appliances but had kept putting it off. He was glad she'd gotten around to replacing them.

Grabbing a beer out of her fridge, he quickly popped the tab and took a huge swig. Today had been one hell of a day and spending a lot of time around Kara hadn't been easy. His parents had to know that, yet it seemed they'd intentionally prolonged the day.

"Virgil?"

"I'm still in the kitchen," he called out. "Want anything?"

"A cold bottle of water would be nice."

"A cold bottle of water coming up," he said, reopening her refrigerator and grabbing a bottle of water. He walked out of the kitchen, stepped into the living room and suddenly stopped. Not only had she changed shoes, she'd also changed clothes.

"Is anything wrong?"

"You changed clothes."

She smiled, glancing down at herself. "Yes, I decided to get comfortable. Anything wrong with what I have on?"

The fact that it wasn't purple was the first thing he noticed, although she did look good in the silky black shirt dress. What he liked most was how it was showing off her legs as well as how the outfit buttoned up the front with a shirttail hem that fanned across her backside. She wasn't wearing a bra, he was sure of it, and for some reason he had a feeling she wasn't wearing panties, either. She was taking "comfortable" to a level he definitely liked.

"No, nothing is wrong with what you're wearing. Here's the water," he said, handing the bottle to her in a way that ensured their hands wouldn't touch. He wasn't sure how much control he would have if they did.

"Thanks."

He watched her uncap the top and tilt the bottle up to her lips. Immediately his gut clenched. It was almost too much temptation. Renewed desire throbbed all through him, nearly overtaking his senses. Knowing he needed to get a grip, he glanced around the room and then said, "I like the changes you made in here."

"Thanks. My next project is removing all this carpet and replacing it with wood floors."

"That will be nice."

"Yes, I think so."

She placed the half-empty water bottle on the coffee table and eased down on the sofa, tucking her feet beneath her. Doing so gave him more than a flash of bare thigh. He could feel the pounding of his heart in his chest.

"You said we needed to talk."

Yes, he had. He settled into the chair across from her, wondering about the best way to approach what he had to say. He figured the best thing to do was to come right out and not beat around the bush. "I want you, Kara. And you want me."

She raised a brow. "You think so? About me wanting you?"

"Yes." He paused a moment and held her gaze. "Are you going to deny it?"

She didn't say anything for a minute, and then she said, "At some point in our lives, Virgil, we all want things we can't have. Things we don't need. Things that can cause us more harm than good. Things that —"

"Don't get all philosophical on me, Kara," he interrupted in a tense voice.

He drew in a deep, shaky breath when his gaze left her face and scanned down her body before returning to her face again. She had a way of stirring up his emotions and passions that could do him in if he wasn't careful. "Just answer the question."

She broke eye contact with him to glance around the room, deliberately looking at everything but him. When she returned her gaze to his, she began nibbling at her lips before she finally spoke. "And if I do want you, Virgil, then what?"

He swallowed against the massive lump in his throat. He could tell her about a lot of ideas he had in mind. And all of them hot, raw and sexual. Instead he said, "Then it's time to present my own action plan."

Kara arched a brow. Virgil was sitting across from her taking another swig of his beer as if giving her time to digest what he'd said. She was doing more than digesting it. Her imagination was going wild with ways she could use whatever action plan he'd come up with to her advantage.

When he had walked out of her kitchen minutes ago, he had stood tall, broad shouldered and sexy. She could remember his muscular chest very well. Remember all the times that naked chest had rubbed against her breasts, causing her nipples to tighten.

"And what if I said I'm not interested?" she asked, studying him intently.

He stretched his long legs out in front of him and his mouth slanted into a sexy and seductive smile. "You haven't heard it yet."

"Don't have to, Virgil. I know how your mind works."

His smile widened and it made her pulse race. "You probably do, but I still want you to hear me out. I think I have a plan where we can both benefit."

She didn't say anything for a long moment. Instead she sat there and continued to hold his gaze. They were looking at each other with unflinching directness, even while she felt waves of sensual heat rippling between them. She could even feel the tightening of her nipples beneath the silk of her dress. And from his position in the chair, she could see the huge bulge pressing hard against the zipper of his pants. He wasn't even trying to hide his erection. Rather he seemed to be intentionally letting her see the proof of what he'd said earlier. He wanted her.

Kara knew Virgil was fully aware of what he was doing to her with his gaze. It was deliberately warming her, caressing her and sending throbbing need shooting through her. She'd discovered long ago that, when it came to seduction, Virgil's gaze was a mesmerizing force to contend with. It had the ability to break down her defenses. But for her it was about more than rolling in the sack a few times. She wanted to be back in his life. Totally and completely. She knew he couldn't fathom such a thing happening, but she had to believe she could pull it off. She was putting her heart on the line. But the big question was, would he ever feel secure enough to put his on the line again?

"Kara?"

"Fine, let's hear it," she said in a tone that made it seem as if she'd gotten annoyed, when in truth she'd gotten aroused just thinking about what he might have in mind. Like she told him, she knew how his mind worked.

He placed his beer can on the table. "I propose we become lovers."

"Why?"

He chuckled and the sound sent sensuous shivers down her spine. "Do you really have to ask me that?"

No, she didn't, but she wanted him to spell it out to her anyway. Every single detail. She needed to hear it. Feel it. Imagine it. "Yes, I think I have to ask. I want to make sure I fully understand what you're proposing, exactly what I'll be getting myself into."

Virgil nodded. "Fair enough." He paused a minute before he continued. "What you'll be getting yourself into, Kara, is me. And I will be getting myself into you. Your action plan requires us to spend a lot of time together for the next several weeks. I see no reason why we can't make it worth our while. We're still attracted to each other so we might as well do something about it. Enjoy each other, both in and out of bed. Mix business with pleasure. Stir up mindblowing passion the way we used to do."

He paused for a moment and Kara knew what his next words would be even before he spoke them. "But be forewarned, Kara. What we share will be sex and nothing else. There will never be anything of substance between us ever again."

"Don't you think I know that, Virgil?"

"Just making sure that you do. I need to be sure you understand that sex is all we can ever share. I have to know you can be satisfied with that."

"Yes, I'd be satisfied because that's the way I'd want it, as well." She could tell he was surprised by her words.

"I'm curious why you feel that way."

She shifted in her seat and watched his gaze move from her face to the glimpse of bare skin on her thighs, just like she had wanted it to do. When his gaze had slid back to her face, she said, "You make it clear how things stand between us every chance you get. I've decided I wouldn't want to get back with you even if the possibility was there."

She forced back her smile from the glare that came into his eyes. "And why is that?"

"Because I could never love a man with such an unforgiving nature. A man who expects me to be perfect, thinks he makes no mistakes, when I know he's certainly made a few of his own."

"You think I want a perfect woman?"

"Doesn't matter what I think. And to be honest I no longer care, Virgil." She eased off the sofa. "Now if you don't mind, it's getting late and I plan to go to early-morning church service tomorrow."

He eased up out of his chair, as well. "So you're in agreement that we should be lovers?"

"I'll think about it and let you know," she said, heading for the door to let him out. She knew he thought he would be staying a little longer, but she would do things on her time and not his.

"When will you let me know?" he asked when he stood across from her in the foyer.

"Soon."

"How soon, Kara?"

She thought he sounded pretty anxious. "Before the end of the week."

He was silent for a minute before saying, "Then maybe I need to leave you with a little persuasion."

"You can try." She knew Virgil Bougard didn't like to be dared.

He reached out and placed his arms around her waist to bring her closer to the fit of him. "I presented you with my action plan, Kara. Now for a sample of that action." And then he lowered his mouth to hers, kissing her with a desperation that made her toes curl and shot arrows of pleasure throughout her body.

When she parted her lips on a breathless sigh, he took advantage of the opportunity and swept his tongue inside her mouth in a smooth delicious stroke. She settled into his kiss, pressing the lower part of her body against him. And when he deepened the kiss, she could feel her heart stir in the pit of her stomach as their tongues tangled, mated voraciously, ravenously and urgently.

He was doing more than giving her a sample. Virgil was trying to erode her senses while kissing her with pure, unadulterated possession. Hadn't he said that any affair between them would be nothing more than sex? Then why was he kissing her as if he intended for her to be a keeper?

He finally broke off the kiss, and then as if he needed to catch his breath, he pressed his forehead against hers. That was good because she definitely needed to catch her breath. But then, before she realized what he was about to do, he eased back and reached out a hand to open the first few buttons of her dress, exposing her breasts. He stood quietly for a moment, not saying anything as his eyes simply feasted on her bare breasts. She felt her nipples harden even more before his gaze.

He reached out and cupped her breasts in his hands, running his fingers across the budded tips. When he lowered his head and sucked a nipple in his mouth, Kara's breathing escalated and she got weak in the knees. Reaching up she grabbed hold of his shoulders for support. And when he licked the nipple he was holding hostage, she forced back a moan.

To her detriment he didn't stop there. Reaching down he finished unbuttoning her dress all the way to the hem to find her naked. Without breaking from his torment of her breasts, he slid his hand between her legs.

Perfect, Virgil thought, when Kara parted her legs for him. When it came to multitasking, he was a pro. With his mouth on her breasts and his hands stroking her between the legs, he was proving just how much of an expert he was. He'd always enjoyed this, priming her with foreplay before getting down to the real business of easing inside her. He would stroke her back and forth, over and over again, while enjoying the sounds of the moans she would make, the way her breathing escalated and her body trembled.

His mouth moved to her other breast, and without letting up, his fingers continued to stroke her below. He loved the sounds of her purrs. It had been a while since he'd heard them and hearing them now made him realize what he'd missed. To be honest, he had missed her. He would admit that. They had been good together and could be good together again. At least this way, which was the only way he wanted. Sex, sex and more sex.

When he heard her groan his name, he knew his fingers were about to push her over the edge and he wanted his tongue to join his fingers when she toppled. He quickly released her breast and dropped to his knees, widening her legs in the process. She screamed the moment his tongue replaced his fingers and he gripped tightly to her thighs while his mouth locked down on her. He greedily began lapping her.

"Virgil!"

And then it happened for her and nothing, not even the feel of her fingernails digging into his shoulders, could make him stop and pull back. He needed her taste like he needed to breathe. It was only when he felt the last spasm pass through her body that he slowly released her thighs and reluctantly pulled his mouth away. But not before getting in one final intense lick. And he couldn't pass up the chance to place several nips around her womanly folds.

Leaning back on his haunches he looked up at her. Holding her gaze, he licked his lips, wanting her to know just how much he'd enjoyed her taste. Her face glowed from the effects of her orgasms and he thought she looked utterly beautiful.

Virgil recalled a time when seeing such a look on her face would make him crazier in love with her, so crazy he couldn't think straight. He blinked and quickly pushed that particular memory from his mind.

Slowly easing up from the floor, he didn't say anything but proceeded to button up her dress, ignoring the way his fingers trembled while doing so. More than once he had to rework a button when it kept coming back open.

When he had refastened all ten buttons he met her gaze and said, "Let me know your decision soon, Kara," in a voice that sounded husky to his own ears. "What we just shared was merely an appetizer. Let me know when you're ready for the full-course meal."

And then, after giving her lips one final lick, he leaned closer and whispered in her ear. "Sleep well tonight."

And then he opened the door and left.

CHAPTER 14

Kara woke up the next morning and for the longest time she just lay there and stared up at the ceiling. Last night had been round one and of course Virgil hadn't played fair. In fact she was convinced he hadn't been playing at all. He was deadly serious in his conquest of her, and all in the name of sex. But then, it didn't take much to recall that's how things had been the last time. He'd started out wanting nothing more than sex from her, but in the end they had fallen in love.

A part of her wanted to believe, had to believe, that it could be that way for them again. Virgil might think he wanted just sex, but it was up to her to show him she wasn't a just-sex kind of woman. Never was and never would be. He had his guard up and would continue to keep it up, but a part of her felt she'd been able to jump the first hurdle.

That meant she had to be on top of her A game because he was definitely on top of his. Even now her body was still stirring in passionate bliss from last night. While standing in the middle of her foyer, he'd taken her breasts, drawing them into his mouth, tugging, laving and sucking on them, torturing them with his tongue. He had pleasured her and made her remember things she had tried to forget. And if that wasn't bad enough, he'd used his mouth between her legs and made her come not once but twice. The man's mouth was definitely a weapon of deadly seduction.

Knowing Virgil, he would expect her to call him today, but she had no plans to do so. Nor would she call him tomorrow or the day after that. He thought the ball was now in his court but he was wrong. She would keep it in hers even if it killed her. It was her intention to let him think about what he was proposing, because if he thought she wouldn't come up with a few plays of her own then he was in for quite a surprise.

"Pam, did you receive that call I'm expecting from Kara Goshay?" Virgil asked his administrative assistant.

"No, sir, not yet. Do you want me to give her a call?"

Although he was tempted to take that option, he said, "No. That's not necessary." It had been three days and as far as he was concerned it was three days too long. He needed her to make a decision but, knowing Kara, she was probably trying to make a mountain out of a molehill. Personally, he didn't see the big deal, especially after what happened at her place Saturday night. She either was for them becoming lovers or not. He had a feeling she was stalling and that was unacceptable.

He glanced up when he heard the knock on his door. "Come in."

He stood when his father walked into his office. "Dad? I thought you and Mom were leaving for Houston today."

"We are but our flight doesn't leave until late this evening," Matthew said, easing into the chair in front of Virgil's desk.

"Would you like a cup of coffee?"

Matthew waved off the offer. "No thanks. Your mom and I had breakfast with Anthony and Claire at the Racetrack Café."

Anthony Lassiter, Uriel's father, was dating Claire Steele, aunt to Mayor Morgan Steele. A few years ago, Anthony's wife of over thirty years had asked for a divorce so she could date younger men. Virgil knew the divorce had left his godfather Anthony emotionally damaged. Virgil was glad he seemed happy now. Anthony and Claire had been seeing each other for about three years now and everyone was hoping for an announcement of something permanent. Evidently a second chance at love was possible for some people.

His father sat forward in the chair, a hand on Virgil's desk. "I understand Ellie is giving Uriel a birthday party next month at the lake and that Winston and Zion are coming home to attend. It will be nice to have all my godsons in one place again. Your mom and I were on that cruise when Winston and Ainsley came home in February."

"Yes, it will be good for all of us to be together. Do you know if all the godfathers will be there, as well?"

"Yes, we all plan to be there."

Virgil nodded. "Good. Then it will be like old times."

When Matthew didn't say anything for a minute, Virgil had a feeling there was something on his father's mind, so he decided to ask. "Dad, is anything wrong?"

Matthew shook his head. "I wouldn't say anything is wrong, Virgil — it's just, your mom and I are concerned."

He arched a brow. "About what?"

"You and Kara. In fact, we're more concerned about Kara than about you."

"What do you mean?"

"What I mean, Virgil, is that when you told us last week that Kara would be the woman you would be seeing exclusively while she worked on improving your image, we had our concerns. And after this weekend, our concerns have increased."

Virgil didn't understand. "What concerns?"

"You and Kara have history and I hope you're not using this as an opportunity to get back at her. To deliberately hurt her like she hurt you."

He remembered Uriel had thought the same thing. "I wouldn't do anything like that," he said, annoyed his parents would think that he would. "My seeing Kara has nothing to do with revenge. She was the most logical woman to make what needs to be done believable."

"I agree, but we don't want you doing anything out of line with her."

Virgil had to fight back the temptation to tell his father that whatever he did to Kara was none of his business. He wasn't a teenager who needed his parents meddling in his affairs. Out of respect, however, he decided to speak his next words carefully, but still make sure his father got the message to back off and let him handle the situation without any interference. When it came to business, because his father was the CEO of Bougard Enterprises, Virgil had no choice but to let him take charge, but when it came to his personal life, Virgil had no problem drawing the line.

"Dad, there's no reason for you and Mom to be concerned about anything that goes on between me and Kara. She knows where we stand and what will never be between us again. She apologized for believing the worst of me and I accepted her apology. We've moved on and we're only pretending interest in each other for Bougard Enterprises' sake."

Matthew nodded. "Your mother and I know what the plan is, but we also saw how you were looking at Kara on Saturday."

Virgil blew out a breath. There was no need to pretend ignorance because he was well aware he'd been caught checking out Kara a few times. "She's a good-looking woman."

"We know that and your mom feels she will make some man a good wife. And since it won't be you, when this is over she intends to introduce Kara to Dr. Alvin Lynwood. Your mother just hopes that the time Kara is spending with you, trying to improve your image, doesn't tarnish her own."

Virgil sat up in his chair. He'd never met Dr. Lynwood but knew he was the man who'd replaced his mother as president of the college when she'd retired. His mother liked the man a lot and had mentioned on more than one occasion what a great job she thought Dr. Lynwood was doing. But Virgil couldn't believe his mother would try setting Kara up with another man. And how could they think being with him could mess up Kara's image?

As if Matthew saw the questions in his eyes, he said, "Your mother sees nothing wrong with introducing Kara to Dr. Lynwood since you've made it known on several occasions there will never be anything between you and her again."

"Yes, but that's not the point."

Matthew frowned. "Then what is the point, Virgil? You've certainly moved on with other women and I'm sure Kara has dated other men since the two of you parted ways four years ago."

"I'm sure none of those men were anyone my mother introduced her to," Virgil said, trying to curtail his anger. "And why would Mom think the time Kara and I are spending together could have any bearing on her image?"

"Think about it, Virgil. I'm sure you've seen the article and photos in *Flo on the Ro* this morning. From the looks of it, Flo's posse was out in full force at the commencement ceremony on Saturday. The two of you are linked back together. That's good news for you, but what happens when, in a month or so, your image has improved and then it appears that you've broken things off with Kara?"

Before Virgil could respond, Matthew stood. "Well, I'd best be going now. Your mom gave me a list of errands to do before we can get to the airport later. We'll text you when we get to Houston to let you know our plane landed safely."

Moments after his father left, Virgil was still sitting behind his desk. How could his mother think about hooking Kara up with Dr. Alvin Lynwood? Didn't the man just get a divorce from his wife sometime last year?

The buzzer on his desk went off. "Yes, Pam?"

"Kara Goshay is on line two."

Virgil ignored the increased beating of his heart. "Thanks."

He quickly went to his second line. "Kara?"

"Virgil. I was wondering if you'd like to

join me for dinner."

Right now he wasn't interested in dinner. He needed an answer to his proposal. "And what about what I suggested to you Saturday night?"

"I'll give you my answer at dinner."

If he thought she was deliberately stalling before, he was even more convinced of it now. "Fine. Where do you want us to meet for dinner?"

"My place at seven. And bring a bottle of wine. Goodbye."

And before he could say anything he heard the definite click in his ear.

Kara glanced down at herself one more time before heading for the door. Virgil had arrived. When she'd called him today, she had decided she'd made him wait long enough for her decision. The goal was to not appear too eager and she would certainly continue that trend tonight.

"Who is it?"

"Virgil."

Dismissing how much she liked hearing the sound of his voice, she steeled herself and then opened the door. The man standing there holding a bottle of wine in his hand nearly took her breath away. How could any man look so insidiously handsome and utterly sexy?

"Kara."

"Virgil."

When she didn't move and just stood there and stared, he smiled and asked, "May I come in?"

Too late she'd realized what she'd been doing. "Yes, of course." Standing aside as he entered, she caught the scent of his aftershave and immediately thought he smelled just as good as he looked.

"Here you are," he said, handing the wine to her.

"Thanks." She walked ahead and said over her shoulder, "I hope you're hungry. I prepared lasagna." She knew how much he loved lasagna, especially hers.

"I can't wait."

And before she knew what he intended to do, he reached out and pulled her to him. "Hey, not so fast," he whispered against her lips. "What have you decided?"

She looked up at him, stared into the penetrating dark eyes. "I'll tell you over dinner."

"I want to know now."

She raised an arched brow. "What's the rush?"

That, Virgil thought, was a good question, and one for which he didn't have an answer.

He had been anxiously awaiting her decision since Saturday and saw no reason for her to delay it any longer. Since she had asked him, he knew the response he could give her that would have credence. Pulling her closer to him, plastering himself against her, he said, "Feel me? Now ask me your question again."

He figured the huge boner practically poking into her pretty much spelled things out for her. They were standing in her foyer again and he had no problem stripping her naked and taking her here and now. Although he liked the outfit she was wearing, a cute floral-print sundress, he'd rather see her wearing nothing at all.

She pushed back from him and smiled. "Okay, I feel you. Let's eat." She walked off and he frowned as he followed her toward the kitchen.

"You know where the bathroom is to wash up," she said, moving over to the stove after setting the wine on the table.

He glanced across the breakfast bar at her, trying not to recall that he'd taken her before right there. She was moving around her kitchen as if she'd completely dismissed him for the time being. Had she forgotten about the screams his fingers and mouth had elicited from her the last time he was here? If so, then maybe he needed to remind her.

Instead of moving in the direction of the bathroom, he moved around the breakfast bar and headed straight toward her. She looked up at him, surprised. "That was quick."

He smiled. She thought he'd washed up already and was definitely wrong about that. Instead of saying anything, he took the spatula out of her hand and placed it on the kitchen counter.

"Virgil? What do you think you're doing?"

Instead of answering, he swept her off her feet and into his arms.

"Put me down!"

Refusing to do what she asked, he headed toward the living room. Once there he eased down on the sofa with her cradled in his arms. Tightening his hold he kept her firmly planted in his lap when she tried to wiggle out of it. "Stay still, will you?"

She glared over at him. "Why should I?"

"For this."

And then he lowered his head and before she could draw her next breath he slanted his mouth across hers. At that moment he needed her taste more than he needed to breathe. As he intended, the kiss was quick, hot but thorough. It got her attention just as he'd meant for it to do.

And now that he had it . . . "So what's it going to be, Kara? Are you willing to accept my terms?"

She surprised him when she leaned up and licked across his lips causing his groin to tighten. She wrapped her arms around his neck and captured his gaze. "It depends."

Her calm response had his gut tightening. "Depends on what?"

"On whether you accept *my* terms."

A funny feeling settled in the pit of his stomach. "And what terms are those?"

She didn't say anything for the longest time and then she finally spoke. "It's a favor, actually. I mentioned to you last week that I would be replacing the carpeting in here with hardwood floors. They're ready to get started. That means I'll need a place to stay for at least a week or two while it's being done. So in other words, Virgil, I need to move in with you."

CHAPTER 15

Kara recognized that look in Virgil's eyes and knew what he was thinking. He'd never shared his space with any woman . . . except for her. And now she was asking him to share it again. And from the hard, penetrating stare he was giving her, he wasn't having it.

"There has to be someplace else you can stay," he said gruffly.

"If there was I wouldn't be asking you" was her quick comeback.

His gaze hardened even more. "What about your sister?"

"I'd rather not. Marti and I aren't on the best of terms."

"Could have fooled me from that day Uriel and I ran into you two at the Race-track Café. You looked pretty chummy then."

"I'd rather not talk about Marti, Virgil. You just have to take my word for it when I say I don't have any place to go."

"Then postpone having your floors done. I'm sure you have that option."

"Yes, but I don't want to take it. Why should I?"

"Because you need somewhere to stay."

He was being a smart-ass. "And you have plenty of room at your place." That was an understatement. In addition to a huge master bedroom, his two-story home that sat on a huge lake had four guest rooms — each with their own full baths — a living room, dining room, family room, eat-in kitchen, a screened-in patio and a three-car garage.

Virgil slid her off his lap and she sat beside him on the sofa. She knew that already he was trying to put distance between them. "I don't share my space, Kara."

She decided not to call him out and say he had once. With her. Although he had never asked her to move in with him permanently, there were a lot of times she'd stayed at his place more than she'd stayed at her own. He'd even given her a key.

"I need you to share your place with me, Virgil."

"No."

"Fine," she said, easing from the sofa. "You need to eat before you leave."

He grabbed her hand before she walked off. "Why, Kara?"

Kara lifted her chin. She knew she was taking a gamble, but she had to break through that solid wall he'd erected. "Like I said, I need a place to stay for just a week or two. You want us to be lovers but I'm not good enough to sleep in your bed."

"You can sleep in my bed all you want, but you can't stay at my place. Temporarily or otherwise."

"Fine. Evidently you don't want me as much as you claim you do. I'll find somewhere else to stay." She tried pulling her hand away but when she did he tugged her back down in his lap.

He tightened his arms around her, and his lips were mere inches from hers when he said in a husky voice, "There's no claiming about it, Kara. I want you."

"Prove it."

Virgil looked at Kara intently for a second. He had no idea what was going on in that pretty little head of hers, but he had no problem proving anything. If she hadn't gotten the message before, then by the time he left tonight, there would be no doubt in her mind about the degree of his desire for her. As far as staying at his place, it wouldn't be happening. There was no way he could handle her invading his space. Not even for one or two weeks.

He drew in a sharp breath when she shifted positions in his lap, causing her backside to rub against his hard, throbbing erection. Heat began building up inside of him. He couldn't resist planting featherlight kisses around her lips before using the tip of his tongue to lick around the edges. She had to feel him harden against her, so how could she think he didn't want her just because he refused to let her move in with him?

"Don't waste my time, Virgil," she said against his mouth. "Either prove it or leave."

He leaned back, held her gaze and his stomach clenched in heated lust. He would prove it all right. "I think dinner will have to hold for a while," he said huskily. Then he stood with her in his arms and headed toward her bedroom.

Kara felt the mattress beneath her back and when Virgil stepped away from the bed, she felt the erratic beat of her heart. She had pushed him and now she knew he wouldn't let her leave this bedroom until he had proven everything to his satisfaction.

As well as to hers.

She'd known exactly what she was doing

in taunting him. Now she had him in a place where she intended to rekindle a lot of hot and steamy memories. By the time he left tonight, she would have proven a few things of her own. Their lovemaking had always been passionate, but they had been pretty emotional, as well. He'd once told her that he'd never made love with a woman until her. Up until then for him it hadn't been anything but sex.

She wanted to believe that the Virgil who had felt that way then would feel that way now. Although he thought her believing the worst about him was unforgivable, a part of her wanted to believe that spending quality time together would eventually wipe away all the hurt and anger. She was taking a big risk, probably the biggest gamble of her life. But she had to believe that what the two of them once shared had been so special there was no way it could have been totally destroyed.

He returned to the bed and before she could blink an eye, he had tugged her up and within seconds had whipped her sundress over her head, leaving her bare except for her panties.

He tossed the dress aside as his gaze scanned her body. It was as if he needed to recapture in his mind what his eyes hadn't feasted on in four years. Granted, he'd tasted her pretty well Saturday evening, but now he was taking his time to look his fill. And she had no problem with that.

Already Kara could feel a deep tingling sensation between her legs. She hadn't slept with another man since Virgil. When she'd thought he had betrayed her, she hadn't wanted to become involved with another man. She'd dated on occasion but could never give her heart or body to anyone else.

"When did you start wearing thongs?" he asked her, intruding into her thoughts. She saw that his gaze was concentrating on the area between her legs and the little scrap of almost nothing lace covering her there.

"Why do you want to know? Do you have a problem with what I have on, Virgil?"

"No. Just curious."

Virgil recalled that she preferred wearing hip-hugging briefs. The thong fit her long legs and curvy hips perfectly and he liked seeing her in it . . . mainly because it exposed more of her body. And speaking of exposure, she wasn't wearing a bra. The last time he'd seen her breasts she hadn't been wearing a bra, either. Had this become a habit?

He shifted his gaze back to her face. "Have you stopped wearing bras?"

"What gave you that idea?"

"This is the second time I've seen you without one."

She smiled. "I don't wear one . . . whenever it suits me."

Hell, it definitely suited him. She had a pair of the lushest breasts any woman could own. Seeing her lying there, tempting and adorably hot, made him want to make love to her real bad. He had to fight hard for control. But then, hadn't she dared him to prove just how much he wanted her?

And he knew just where to start. Reaching out, he lifted her hips and slid the thong down her legs. After tossing it aside, Virgil felt his guts twist into knots as his gaze raked over her entire body. Never had he seen a woman more beautifully made. His fingers trembled when he touched her skin. It felt soft and smooth, almost like velvet. He could recall the days, right after they'd broken up, when his body had gone through withdrawal just thinking how perfect she was and how much he'd wanted her.

He pushed those memories to the back of his mind. That was then. This was now and she was here. He was here and for whatever reason they were back together in this place. He forced the thought that it was a temporary arrangement to the back of his mind.

Right now he didn't care. All he could think about was that he was actually touching her again.

"Virgil?"

He lifted his head and met her gaze. "Yes?"

"What are you waiting on? Christmas?"

He couldn't help but throw his head back and laugh. Only she could make him laugh at a time like this. She always had the ability to keep things lively in the bedroom. "That mouth of yours will get you in trouble," he said, stepping back to start removing his clothes.

"Then I suggest you use that mouth of yours to keep me out of trouble."

"Mmm, I like you naughty," he said, sliding his pants down his legs and liking the look of appreciation in her eyes when she gazed at his erection. That look reminded him of times when she'd definitely been naughty.

Returning to the bed, he sat beside her, needing to touch her some more. As much as he wanted her, and no matter what she said, he would not be rushed into pleasuring her. For some reason, their first mating after all this time needed to be slow and painstakingly meticulous. It might annoy her at first, but in the end she would appreciate it.

He held her gaze as he began stroking between her legs with methodical detail, letting his fingers recall every inch of her, reacquainting his hands with the feel of her and needing to see the play of emotions crossing her face as he did so.

Virgil always thought she was the most passionate of women and pleasuring her had always been an honor as well as a privilege for him. He'd never felt that way with any other woman. Kara could arouse him to unprecedented heights. Even now her feminine scent was enveloping him, eliciting a need that all but crackled with the highest voltage of sexual energy.

He loved the sounds she made while he was getting her ready for what was to come. He wanted her to feel the heat, to desire it and need it as much as he did. His gaze was transfixed on her as he continued to stroke her and he wondered if she detected an air of shimmering sensuality surrounding them.

"Virgil . . ."

It had been a while since he'd heard his name whispered from her lips just that way. He'd missed hearing it. He leaned close to whisper, while keeping his fingers planted between her legs. "Tell me what you want, Kara."

"You."

Sexual tension thickened the blood in his veins and a rush of desire seized his groin. At that moment he couldn't hold back any longer. He had to have her.

Grabbing his pants off the floor, he retrieved a condom packet from his wallet and quickly sheathed himself, knowing she was watching him. Easing back onto the bed, he slid his body in place over hers while gazing down at her.

Needing to touch her, he reached up and tangled his hands with hers by the sides of her face, fighting deep emotions that tried resurfacing. He simply refused to let them. "I'm about to prove just how much I want you, Kara," he whispered when the hard ridge of his erection fit snugly at the entrance of her womanly core.

As if she couldn't wait any longer, she lifted her hips and he slid inside her. He kept going until he was totally embedded and couldn't go any farther. In the past, with him planted so deep inside of her and staring deep into her eyes, he would tell her how much he loved her, and he would feel the very existence of those words deep in his soul. But he was convinced all he was feeling now was the stirring sensations of heated lust combined with sexual excitement curling around in his stomach. There was no way he could love her again. He was convinced of it. But tonight he intended for the sex between them to be good.

Nothing, Kara thought, could ever equate to the feeling of being taken by Virgil. Nothing could compare to the feel of his engorged erection sliding inside of her all the way to the hilt. And then there were the sinfully erotic movements of his hips as he began thrusting hard. The steady rhythm rocked through her veins. She could even feel a throb of desire in the hands holding hers hostage near her head.

And when Virgil increased the pace, making his thrusts even more powerful, she couldn't stop herself from moaning his name. The intensity of their lovemaking was tripping her pulse, sending her heart rate off kilter and setting every inch of her skin on fire. And the look in his eyes held raw, sexual heat.

Then she felt it. The beginning of a thrumming sensation started low in her belly, compressing her inner muscles, making them clench him tight and begin milking him all the way into her womb.

That's when he lowered his head and kissed her, using his tongue to make swirling strokes inside her mouth. She pulled her hands free to grab hold of his shoulders, needing to feel her fingers digging into his muscles. An explosion erupted inside her that shook her, had her bucking her body upward at the same time he shouted her name and slammed downward in one deep, powerful thrust.

He kept kissing her, taking the kiss deeper while thrusting inside of her, running his hands all over her as if he needed to touch her, make sure she was real and not a figment of his imagination. And she kissed him back, needing him as much as he seemed to need her.

He was back in her bed. It would be up to her to make sure passion prevailed over caution, desire superseded Virgil's unforgiving nature and love conquered all.

What the hell happened?

Virgil slumped down beside Kara, totally spent, feeling raw, his muscles unable to function, and his emotions totally exposed. Why did making love to her always leave him with a feeling he couldn't explain? And how, after all this time and everything that had transpired between them, could he feel that way?

He thought that he could make love to her, desire her, yet keep a part of himself detached. But Kara had a way of making him give all or nothing. He'd given his all, and with each and every thrust into her going deep into familiar territory, emotions he'd tried holding at bay — the same ones he'd convinced himself were nonexistent where she was concerned — had overtaken him. In the end, he'd been powerless to fight it. Why?

He quickly concluded the reason had everything to do with being back inside of her after all this time. That coupled with the fact that over the past few weeks he'd been horny as hell. Yes, that had to be the reason why he'd lost it, and why even now he was getting aroused all over again.

Although he was no longer lying on top of her, their limbs were still entwined and his arms were thrown over her waist while they faced each other. She was breathing deeply and her eyes were open, but instead of looking at him she was staring beyond him at a painting on her wall.

So far she hadn't said anything. He couldn't help wondering what she was thinking. Did she regret letting him make love to her? Or, like him, was she thinking what they'd shared had been so mind-blowingly perfect, it had left them both at a loss for words?

He continued to lie there and gaze at her. She had to know he was staring yet she wouldn't look at him. That was fine since he needed to get his mind back on track, although that wouldn't be an easy thing to do. Not when he was thinking about how good it was to lie here beside her like this. He'd always enjoyed this, the aftermath, when they would lie naked in each other's arms and savor what they'd done together. They would talk, more times than not, and confess their love for each other. Telling her the first time that he loved her had been hard because he hadn't spoken those words to any woman before. But after he did it, and knowing she was so deserving of his love, the words had flowed easily and had come frequently . . . especially whenever they made love. For him it had been important that she know he was not confusing love with lust and that he knew the difference.

Tonight had brought back memories of how it felt being inside her, feeling her inner muscles squeeze to clench him and then proceed to milk him dry. She had a way of doing that perfectly, getting every single drop out of him. He had to force back the growl in his throat just thinking about it.

Virgil literally held his breath when Kara

shifted her gaze to look at him. He was certain he wasn't mistaken about the look of total sexual fulfillment he saw in her eyes.

He held tight to her gaze and asked, "You okay?"

Instead of answering him, she reached out and caressed the side of his face and smiled softly. Then she finally said, "Yes. I'm okay. I had to take a minute to get myself together. What we did just now felt simply amazing."

Virgil would have to agree with her and was about to tell her so when she leaned in and placed her mouth over his. He needed this kiss just as much as she apparently did. Possibly even more. And when her tongue entered his mouth he greedily captured it with his own. Their tongues mated for the longest time before she finally lifted her mouth from his.

He was totally aroused all over again and from the way her hands began stroking him, so was she. "I want you again," he whispered, straddling her body and gazing down into her face.

"And more than anything, Virgil, I want you to want me" was her soft response.

He pushed to the back of his mind the possibility that she meant anything by what she'd said. Instead he turned his entire focus, his full concentration on making love to her again.

CHAPTER 16

It looks as if Virgil Bougard is trying to turn over a new leaf. About time. He was seen this weekend with his sleeves rolled up at his company's back-to-school charity event. I might be wrong but it looked like he was enjoying himself while giving out those book bags to all those kids. Can we credit his on-again love affair with Kara Goshay for his change of attitude? Stay tuned.

Kara tossed the newspaper aside to take another sip of her coffee. Thanks to Flo's article in the paper that morning, the strategy to improve Virgil's image was definitely off to a good start. And the photograph of him surrounded by some of the kids who'd attended the book-bag giveaway was priceless. He didn't look like an ordinary executive but, rather, like one who cared. And a part of her truly believed he did. Just like a part of her believed what they'd shared in her bed last week had meant something to him . . . although from the look of things, he'd run scared again.

Getting out of her chair, she took another sip of her coffee as she walked over to the window in her office and gazed out, remembering that night. After making love two more times they'd dressed and gone downstairs to eat the dinner she'd prepared. By then it was after midnight, but she doubted either of them cared. They had worked up a voracious appetite and the lasagna, tossed salad and strawberry cheesecake had hit the spot. He had offered to help clean up the kitchen but she declined his offer. However, he had refused to leave without helping her clear off the table. That was when he'd mentioned he would be out of town for a few days. Without saying when they would see each other again or whether he'd changed his mind about her moving in with him, he had kissed her goodbye and left.

That had been nearly a week ago, and she hadn't heard from him till an hour ago. Out of the blue he'd called to ask her out to dinner. When she'd informed him that tonight wouldn't be good for her because she was in the process of moving out of her condo, he'd said nothing for a minute before saying he would touch base with her later this week. He hadn't even asked where she would be moving to.

Since there was no doubt in her mind that making love with her had meant more to him than just a roll between the sheets, she believed he was fighting it. She couldn't force from her mind how he'd looked down at her, deep into her eyes, when he'd positioned his body over hers. Although Virgil refused to utter the words of love he'd once said, she had felt his resolve breaking with every stroke into her body. Why did he have to be so stubborn, unforgiving and determined not to put his heart on the line again?

She had taken tomorrow off to get settled into the hotel where she would be staying for the next two weeks. There was a lot on her plate and she hoped she would be too busy to think about Virgil.

When Virgil pulled into Kara's driveway he saw several lights were still on, including the one in her upstairs bedroom. He had intentionally not contacted her for almost a week, feeling the need to put distance between them. Making love to her had affected him more than he'd figured it would and he'd needed time away from her to screw his head back on right.

But that hadn't stopped him from going to bed each night thinking of her, wanting her and desiring her in a way he could never desire any other woman. It had taken him all those restless and sleepless nights to figure out that even after four years, Kara wasn't out of his system like he thought and making love to her last week had only complicated matters.

He hadn't wanted to remember how good things used to be when they'd been together but he couldn't help doing so. Nor did he want to think about how, after playing several games of tennis with Donovan Steele, he had rushed home to come here. He couldn't hold out any longer. He wanted to see her again. He *needed* to see her again. He wanted to kiss her. Taste her all over. Make love to her again.

He'd suggested they have an affair and although they'd made love, she hadn't consented to his terms. Instead she'd asked a favor of him, one he'd quickly turned down. Now he wasn't sure where they stood and he needed to find out.

No matter what her ultimate decision would be about the affair, they would still have to be seen together in public for a few more weeks. He, more than anyone, would feel the sting of having to be around her and pretend romantic interest in a woman he wanted to take to bed.

At least he'd spoken to his mother earlier today and convinced her to drop the crazy idea of introducing Kara to Dr. Lynwood. Although he could tell his mother had not seen his point, since nothing serious would ever develop between him and Kara again, she'd agreed to leave it alone.

He had left his parents' home somewhat satisfied and had convinced himself all the way to the tennis courts that his visit with his mother had nothing to do with any jealousy he'd felt. He just didn't want to think about Kara with any other man after him. He knew it didn't make sense but since Kara had reentered his life nothing he did seemed to make much sense anymore.

Like the decision he'd made that morning . . .

It had taken him a while to come around, but he had convinced himself of the merits of having her at his place. That would be a logical move, especially since the two of them were pretending to be exclusive lovers. And he would get what he wanted. Lover's rights. He would go to bed with her and wake up with her. In other words, they would have access to sex whenever they wanted it. And with Kara he had a tendency to want it all the time. He would just have to be diligent in making sure he didn't start thinking with the wrong head. Not the one aching in his jeans at this very moment, but the one attached to his neck. He had to remember that whatever he and Kara shared was short-term and nothing more.

Getting out of the car and closing the door behind him, he headed for her door.

Kara was on her way down the stairs when she heard the ringing of her doorbell. She didn't have to wonder who was at her door. The deep pounding in her chest gave the identity of her visitor away. Why was Virgil here? To help pack up her things for her move to the hotel? A booty call? The thought of the latter caused a heat to stir in the pit of her stomach. She really should be upset that sex was the only thing to bring him here, but pathetic as it might sound, she wanted to believe that making love to her would eventually come to mean something to him again.

She opened the door and stepped aside for him to enter. "Virgil, how was your trip?"

"Productive."

She thought he smelled fresh. And when he strolled by she picked up the scent of his aftershave and thought it was a turn-on.

Instead of stopping in the foyer, he kept walking to her living room. She followed and saw him staring at her packed luggage.

She went over to the sofa and sat down, crossing her legs. "Any reason you're here?"

He moved his gaze to her, especially to her legs, which were exposed because of the short skirt she was wearing. Every time his eyes moved up and down her body, she could feel the sensual pull between them. "I had wanted to take you to dinner."

"And I told you what I'd be doing. Didn't you believe me?"

He shoved his hands into his pockets. "Yes, I believed you. In fact I came by to see if you needed my help."

"No thanks."

"You sure?"

"Positive."

Why did he have to stand over there, looking so perfectly male? And why was she looking at his sensuous mouth and recalling how it could take hers, make love to it, mate with it as if it was something he had every right to do?

He walked over to where she sat and he came to a stop right in front of her. She couldn't miss his aroused state. The huge bulge pressing hard against the zipper of his jeans was something that definitely caught her attention. And then he said in a voice that was deep and husky, "I want you."

She fixed her mouth to tell him the last thing she needed was for him to make a booty call now, but the words couldn't part from her lips. He was still fighting her, battling with emotions. Only someone who'd known him as well as she had could detect the struggle. Even now, he didn't want to want her, but something was driving him to do so anyway.

She knew how Virgil's mind worked. He stood there with his focus directly on her, trying to figure out why he wanted her so much. Why, considering their history, he wanted to strip her naked and make love to her, right where she sat. There was a dark intensity in the depths of his gaze, and the lines around his mouth were deep and drawn. She wondered if he was remembering the night they'd made love, right here in this house, under this roof. Of the time he had dropped to his knees, in the middle of her foyer and tasted her.

Kara was remembering those things and had to believe he was remembering them, as well. She had to believe this wasn't just another booty call but that it was one with a purpose. One that could bring her closer to her goal of cracking through the wall he'd erected around his heart.

She slowly eased from the sofa and stood in front of him, so close their bodies touched. She could feel his hard erection pressing against her middle. Just as she was certain that he could feel the hard buds of her nipples pressing into his chest.

At that moment she decided that although he'd made the booty call, she would be the one to take ownership of it.

"So you think you want me, Virgil?"

From the arch of his brow she knew her question surprised him. Evidently he figured any other woman would take what he'd said without question. In the end he would see she wasn't just any other woman. She was the one who loved him. The one he'd once loved. The one who was fighting hard to regain that love.

"I know I want you, Kara."

Hearing the words spoken so huskily from his lips should have been enough for her but it wasn't. She was fighting to hear him say different words, words that went deeper than just desire. "I'm glad you want me. Now let me show you just how much I want you."

She tugged her blouse over her head and shimmied seductively out of her skirt. And before he could catch his next breath, she reached out and whisked his T-shirt over his head.

Virgil's gaze scanned Kara as she stood there in a skimpy pair of panties. Evidently this was one of those times it suited her since she wasn't wearing a bra. Honestly, she didn't need one. Her breasts were beautiful, firm and full. While he watched, she slid out of her panties.

He was convinced there was not another woman with this much sensuality who walked the face of this earth. Would there always be this sensuous pull between them? One so strong it could create such an intense yearning that it threatened his control? And then there was her gutsiness. It had a way of increasing sexual tension between them to the point where he wanted nothing more than to make love to her all night and most of the next day — nonstop.

She pulled his belt through the loops of his jeans and tossed it aside; however, what made him get harder was when she slowly eased down his zipper. "Take off your jeans, Virgil."

Virgil had no problem doing what she asked and quickly kicked off his shoes and removed his socks before lowering the jeans down his legs. When he tucked his fingers into the waistband of his briefs to tug them down his legs, as well, she placed her hand on his. "I can manage from here."

He nodded as he fixed his gaze on the lushness of her mouth, and he couldn't fight the heat that flared inside him when she licked her lips. And when she knelt in front of him and began easing his briefs down, he swore he could feel the floor beneath his feet shift. Awareness of what she was about to do filled his every pore with sexual greed. Even the air he was breathing seemed to thicken.

When she darted her tongue out of her mouth to moisten the head of his erection, it provoked a deep pounding right there in his crotch. He knew the shape and fullness of her lips, knew what her mouth was capable of doing, and he prepared himself for what was to come. No sooner had that thought entered his mind than she opened her mouth and took him all in. His breath caught while his entire body began to sizzle. He reached out and buried his fingers in her hair and released a torturous moan when a surge of hot, sharp sensation rushed through him.

Then she began sucking on him, just the way she'd done in all his dreams. Just the way she used to do when they'd been a couple. Just the way she knew he liked. Desire twisted his gut and every nerve in his body flared with the intensity of what she was doing. He could feel his erection enlarging and throbbing right in her mouth. She didn't let up and at the rate she was going, he would soon shatter into pieces. But he wanted to be inside of her when he did. And he wanted to be looking into her eyes when their bodies joined.

Ignoring her protest, he reached down and pulled her up and together they tumbled to the sofa. To cushion the impact he made sure she landed on top, straddling him.

She glanced down, flashed him a sexy smile and said, "Perfect landing."

Quickly taking advantage of their positions, she opened her legs wider and lowered her body down onto his shaft. Staring up at her, he gritted his teeth, but that didn't stop the moan from escaping. And when she began riding him, emotions he'd conditioned himself not to feel ripped through him and he grabbed her tight. This wasn't the first time they'd made love on her sofa, but it was the first time they'd done so with her on top.

Every bone in his body quivered with each and every erotic movement of her hips. He felt sexual sensations in every pore, every nerve. When frissons of heat raced up his spine he cupped the back of her head and lowered her mouth down to his. He needed this kiss as much as he needed everything else she was doing to him. The taste of her consumed him while at the same time thickening the blood in his veins.

And when sensations of a magnitude he'd never confronted before seemed to slam into both of them at the same time, they were pushed over the edge together. He had to hold on and maintain balance for the both of them, otherwise they would have tumbled to the floor. She broke her mouth free of his and screamed his name, and the sound seemed to pulverize every bone in his body.

He could feel his release exploding inside her, jetting all the way to her womb. It occurred to him then that he wasn't wearing a condom, and he hoped like hell she was still on the pill. But at that moment he didn't want to think about any possible risks of an unplanned pregnancy. He just wanted to think about how she'd made him feel.

They lay there as pleasure continued to flow through them, even when they were too tired to move. He loved her nakedness and gently stroked her back. Moments later she finally lifted her head to gaze down at him.

"You need to leave. I still have a lot of packing to do," she whispered in a tone he didn't think was too convincing. Not when he could feel himself getting hard inside of her again.

"I told you I would help."

"I don't want your help, Virgil."

"Tough," he said, leaning up and swiping his tongue across the pout that had formed on her lips. "Oh, and I forgot to mention that you're moving in with me."

CHAPTER 17

Kara stretched out her legs and when they came into contact with a muscular and hairy one, she recalled where she was and whose bed she was in. She slowly opened her eyes as memories from last night assailed her. After making love a second time at her place, that time in her bed, she and Virgil had dressed and he had helped her finish packing. It was way past midnight when they'd arrived at his home. By then she was too exhausted to unpack anything. Not even a nightgown.

They had showered together and he'd given her one of his T-shirts to sleep in. For all the good it had done. Once in his bed, he'd immediately taken the shirt off her. And they'd made love again. That was probably why he was still sleeping beside her. She glanced over at the clock, saw it was past eight and hoped he didn't have any meetings planned at the office this morning.

She snuggled back up to him as a feeling of happiness washed over her. A part of her truly believed that no matter what Virgil said or how much he wanted to deny it, he loved her. The fact that she was here, under his roof, in his bed and nestled in his arms spoke volumes. She was certain he still thought it was about nothing more than sex, but she knew better and would be patient until he realized that fact, as well. There were still a lot of roads they would have to travel, more mountains they would need to climb. Trust and faith had to be rebuilt, but she believed they could do it and would do everything within her power to show Virgil that they could, as well. It would take one step at a time.

She believed being here with him this way was a start. It was more than what she'd had a few weeks ago. Even when she remembered his attitude toward her six months ago and where she was now, it was almost akin to a miracle. Somehow she had managed to put a crack in his wall of defense, but that wasn't good enough. She wouldn't be totally satisfied until that wall came tumbling down.

Still feeling totally exhausted, she closed

her eyes when sleep overtook her again.

Virgil awakened to Kara's scent. It surrounded him and he would be surprised if it hadn't permeated his skin. He liked it. Always had. And the thought that she was here in his bed was simply unreal.

He glanced down at her. She was snuggled close to his side with their legs entwined. Her head was resting on his chest and one of her arms was thrown across his midsection. It was like déjà vu, reliving how things used to be, on those mornings when he would wake up beside her. Things could never be that way again so he would enjoy this while it lasted.

He glanced over at the clock and was glad he'd cleared his calendar for the morning. Besides, he needed to work on that proposal for Stan Nelson, the wealthy Canadian who'd come highly recommended by a college classmate and friend. He'd been courting the Nelson Group for almost a year now and when he'd met with the man this week in Toronto, Virgil had felt it was almost a done deal. But he wasn't ready to mention it to anyone just yet. Not even to his father. He figured pulling something like this off would definitely make his dad a happy man. Hopefully happy enough to actually retire this time. And what Virgil liked about Nelson was that the man — who was known as a womanizer — didn't give a damn about Virgil's reputation. He wanted a man he could trust his money with.

Virgil knew he had to keep the deal quiet until everything was finalized, which hopefully would be in a couple of weeks. He glanced down at Kara again. On the drive here he had asked if she was still on the pill and had been relieved to find out she was. But then why had the image of a little girl with her features flashed through his mind?

As much as he wanted to wake Kara up so they could make love again, he knew he couldn't. She needed her rest. He glanced around the room and his eyes lit on her luggage, which he'd brought in after she'd fallen asleep. For someone who was only staying a week or so, she'd certainly packed a lot of stuff. But then, he would have to admit he didn't know of any woman who traveled light.

There were a few calls he needed to make this morning, so he slowly detached himself from Kara and eased out of bed. Already he felt a sense of loss with their bodies no longer connected. Grabbing his bathrobe off a chair he slid it over his naked body, remembering every single detail about the times they'd made love at her place and his. Before heading for the bathroom, he glanced back over at Kara and put the thought out of his mind that she looked as though she belonged in his bed.

Kara awoke and she pulled herself up in bed to find she was alone. Where had Virgil gone? The smell of coffee was a dead giveaway. He had to have a cup first thing in the morning while he read the newspaper.

Easing out of bed, she couldn't help but smile when she saw he'd brought all her luggage into his bedroom. Last night they had left everything downstairs, and although she had slept in his bed, she wasn't sure if that's how things would be or if he would expect her to use one of his guest rooms. It seemed he'd made the decision for her to share this room with him.

When she heard her cell phone, she quickly rushed across the room to dig it out of her purse. She answered, not recognizing the caller ID. "Hello?"

"Where are you? I stopped by your place this morning and a group of workers were there. They said you had moved out to have some work done on your floors."

Kara eased into the wingback chair upon hearing her sister's voice. She hadn't talked to Marti since the day they'd had breakfast together at the Racetrack Café. Kara was trying hard to find it in her heart to forgive Marti and move on, but each time she tried doing so, she had a funny feeling about something that wouldn't go away.

"Why did you stop by my place?" Although she'd never told Marti she wasn't welcome there anymore, she certainly hadn't invited her sister over, either.

"To invite you to lunch and to give you my new cell number."

Marti had had her old cell number for years. "Why did you change it?"

"I started getting weird calls from a man I didn't know. Not sure how he got my number so I decided to change it."

Kara's concern for her sister kicked in. No matter what, she loved her and didn't want anything to happen to her. "Did you report it to the police?"

"No. Hopefully, changing my phone number will do the trick. If not, I'll go to the cops." There was a pause and then Marti asked, "So where are you? If you needed a place to stay, you could have crashed here with me."

Kara knew there was no way she could have done that. "Thanks, but I'm living with Virgil for a while."

"He's letting you do that?"

Kara raised a brow. Why was there surprise in Marti's voice? As far as Marti and anyone else knew — except for Virgil's parents and possibly his godbrothers — they had gotten back together.

"And why wouldn't he, Marti? Virgil and I are back together again." The lie was part of their ruse, but she couldn't help hoping it would eventually be true.

"No reason. Well, you have my number now. I hope we can do lunch soon."

Maybe they should. She didn't like the thought of Marti having to change her phone number because of harassing calls. "Yes, let's. I'll call you next week and we can plan something then."

"Thanks, Kara. I'll await your call."

Virgil turned from the stove when he heard Kara enter his kitchen, trying not to remember what happened the last time she'd done so. He remembered as if it had been yesterday. He was doing the same thing then that he was doing now, which was fixing breakfast, when he'd turned around. Instead of being fully dressed like she was now, she'd opted to wear just his dress shirt, unbuttoned, with nothing else on underneath. He recalled sweeping her into his arms to carry

251

her back upstairs, but they hadn't made it that far and had ended up making love on the stairs.

"Something smells good."

He started to tell her that she smelled good. Frying bacon had nothing on her. He'd also liked her scent right before they'd made love. It was always a good indication of when she wanted it as much as he did.

"I wondered when the smell of bacon would bring you down here. It's almost lunchtime."

"I noticed, and why aren't you at work?"

"I decided to play hooky today and hang out with you."

Kara liked the sound of that. She tried not to notice how good Virgil looked shirtless, shoeless and with a pair of jeans riding low on his hips. He was one sexy man who knew his way around the kitchen, thanks to two grandmothers who knew the meaning of good food.

"If you do, then I'll put you to work helping me unpack."

He laughed. "You're not afraid I might see all that girly stuff?"

"Nothing you haven't seen before, although I have picked up some new things over the years." She thought about the purple negligee she'd recently purchased.

"Like those thongs?"

She chuckled. "Yes, like those thongs. You like them, don't you?"

He leaned against the kitchen counter while his gaze roamed all over her as if he had X-ray vision to see beyond her jeans and top. "Yes, I like them. Go on and sit down. Breakfast is almost ready."

"You didn't have to cook breakfast for me, you know," she said, doing what he said by taking a seat at his table. The same one she had helped him pick out when he'd decided to replace his last one. She loved his kitchen since it had a good view of a golf course and lake. "And don't you dare try to convince me it's something you do all the time because I know you don't," she added.

"You're right. But I knew how much you like grits, scrambled eggs and bacon and decided after all we did last night, you deserved energy food," he said, bringing several platters over to the table.

"That was kind of you."

He smiled when he joined her at the table. "It's the least that I can do." And he meant it. He'd been a greedy ass last night as far as her body was concerned, and although he'd made sure she got her pleasure, as well, he had kept her from getting a good night's sleep.

"By the way, I noticed your phone ringing a couple times while I was shaving. You were sleeping so soundly, I didn't wake you. I hope you didn't miss an important call."

The missed calls had been from Marti, and Kara decided mentioning her sister right now wasn't a good idea. "No, it wasn't important."

She hadn't realized just how hungry she was until she began eating. They shared conversation over breakfast and Kara was surprised how relaxed and unguarded Virgil appeared to be around her, and she was grateful for that.

After breakfast she helped him with the dishes and then they went upstairs to unpack her things. Of course they got waylaid several times, with several showers in between. What should have taken them less than an hour ended up taking them all afternoon.

She offered to cook dinner but he suggested they go out instead. They decided to go back to the Goldenrod. They both agreed the food had been delicious the last time they'd gone there. And just like before, they enjoyed their meal. After dinner he took her by her place to pick up a few items she had forgotten to pack.

Before returning to Virgil's place they had

dropped by his parents' home to check on things while the older couple were in Houston. Virgil and Kara arrived back at his place, and no sooner had the door closed behind them than Virgil pulled her into his arms and kissed her with the passion of a man who enjoyed what he was doing. And she proved to him she appreciated all the attention. Later that night while he held her in his arms, a satisfied Kara thought the day had been simply wonderful and wished their remaining days together would be just as special.

She had only two weeks to completely tear down the wall Virgil had built around his heart.

CHAPTER 18

Xavier Kane leaned back in his chair and studied the man sitting across the table from him at the Racetrack Café. "You've certainly been in a good mood lately, V."

Virgil glanced up from his plate. "Have I?"

"Yes."

"Just your imagination."

"Um, I don't think so. Uriel mentioned it, as well. So did Winston. Although, he did say when he called last week you rushed him off the phone."

"Like you, he's imagining things," Virgil said, taking a sip of his coffee. "And when is Bronson's next race? I think I'm —"

"Don't try changing the subject. I want to know why you're in such a good mood. You have a tendency to be an ass at times, although you don't curse as much as you used to. If I didn't know better I'd think . . ."

Xavier didn't finish what he was about to

say. He merely stared at Virgil.

"You'd think what?"

"That you and Kara are back together — for real, and not for any pretense."

Virgil pushed his plate aside and leaned back in his chair. "But I hope you do know better."

Xavier chuckled. "Can't say that I do. Couples are known to get back together. Farrah and I did. So did Uriel and Ellie. York and Darcy. Winston and Ainsley."

"I'm happy for all of you but that has nothing to do with me."

"I understand Kara has moved in with you."

He didn't have to wonder how Xavier knew that. Uriel had dropped by his place and Kara had been there. "Doesn't mean anything. I'm sure the person who told you that she was there also mentioned it's only temporary."

"Yes, he did mention it, but . . ."

"But what?"

"Like I said, you've been in a good mood. Maybe Kara should become a permanent fixture at your place."

"That won't be happening. She has another week and then she's out of there."

"You sure?"

"Just as sure as I know my father's name

is Matthew and my mom's name is Rhona."

"I hope you aren't making a big mistake."

"I'm not. Now will you tell me when Bronson's next race is?" He told himself he wasn't changing the subject, that he just wanted to ensure he didn't miss his friend's car race.

An hour later while driving back to his office, Virgil thought about his conversation with Xavier. So what if he'd been in a good mood lately? Was that a crime? And although he wouldn't admit it to Xavier or anyone else, Kara *was* responsible.

Virgil tightened his hands on the steering wheel. The last thing he needed was to fill his mind with foolish thoughts. He and Kara were having no more than an affair. He had affairs all the time so why should this one be any different? It was different because he was her client. He couldn't lose sight of the fact that this was a job for her — a job that she was getting paid to do with the goal of improving his image. Not one to miss an opportunity, he'd simply capitalized on a good thing and he had no regrets about doing so.

If he was telling the truth, he would also admit that the thought of her returning to her place in a week didn't actually fill him with joy. He'd gotten used to waking up with her in his arms, her leg thrown over his or his over hers. Making love to her in the mornings and going to sleep after making love to her at night. Sharing breakfast and dinner with her. Being seen around town with her. It was beginning to feel just like old times —

He stopped himself right there. That was the one thing he couldn't allow to happen. Those days were over and done with. He'd told Kara that, and as far as he was concerned she had no reason not to believe him.

But what if she thought he'd changed his mind? What if she'd gotten it in her head that they could be a couple again just because they were enjoying each other in and out of bed? He hoped she hadn't, because she'd be in for a rude awakening if that was the case. As soon as her house was ready, she would be returning to it.

"You truly look happy, Kara."

Kara glanced over at Marti. They were enjoying lunch at her sister's condo. This was the first time she'd been here since finding out what Marti had done. She couldn't help smiling over at her sister. "I am happy."

"Because of Virgil?"

She held her sister's gaze. "Yes, because of Virgil. I know you don't like talking about what you did four years ago, Marti, but in order for our relationship to move forward, you truly need to regret what you did, and I don't honestly think that you do."

"I apologized, didn't I?"

"Yes, but was it sincere? I'm not sure it was."

Marti looked down and didn't say anything for a long time. Then she met Kara's gaze and said softly, "I honestly thought Virgil would hurt you, Kara, and I couldn't let him do that. I've been out there a lot longer than you have. I know the players, the heartbreakers, the men women trust only to find out how wrong they are, the men who don't mean a woman any good. And I didn't like the thought that one of those had targeted you."

"But Virgil changed while we were together. Surely you could see that."

"Yes, but still. I couldn't risk my kid sister getting hurt by a man the way I was."

Kara didn't say anything as she saw the pain in Marti's eyes, pain she was seeing for the first time, which meant her sister had done a good job of hiding it over the years. "Tell me about him," she coaxed.

When Marti shook her head, Kara reached out and took her hand. "You have to tell me. Maybe telling me will not only cleanse yourself of him but also help me to understand."

Marti didn't say anything for a minute, as if she was debating whether to share her story. "His name was Malcolm Edwards," she said finally. "He was already living in Sacramento when I moved there after college. I was twenty-four. Young. Naive. Too trusting. And my head was filled with romantic ideas of love and forever after. Why wouldn't it be? Our parents loved each other and set a good example for us to follow. So naturally, I assumed that one day I would marry a man who loved me and I would have his children. I'd heard about Malcolm's reputation with women, but when we were together he made me feel special. And I honestly thought he had fallen in love with me. Like you and Virgil, we dated for almost a year. Things were going great and I definitely wasn't prepared for what he did."

Kara's heart pounded in her chest. "What did he do?"

Kara could see the pain in her sister's eyes deepen. "One night he had four of his closest friends over to watch a football game. We hadn't moved in together yet, but I figured it was only a matter of time since I was spending more time at his place than my own."

After a momentary pause Marti continued. "I knew about the football game and since none of the guys brought their girlfriends, I figured I would hang out in the bedroom and study for my CPA exam."

Kara watched her sister and knew she was fighting back tears. She wanted to reach out and take her hand, but she remained still, letting Marti set the pace.

"I honestly don't know what happened. The only thing I remember was Malcolm coming into the bedroom and offering me a glass of wine. He said I was studying too much and it would relax me. I thanked him for being thoughtful and drank it. Everything else is kind of woozy after that. All I remember is waking up sometime during the night in bed with five men. And I could tell from the way my body felt that all five of them had taken turns with me."

"They raped you?"

Marti wiped a tear from her eyes. "Yes. And just to make sure I knew what they had done, when they saw I was awake, they raped me again."

She stared with teary eyes at Kara. "Malcolm watched while his friends gagged my mouth and tied up my hands and had their way with me before he took his turn. He said he and his best friends shared every-thing."

Kara was indignant, angry beyond belief. "Did you call the police?"

"That's what's so sad. One of them was a cop. And he threatened to do all kinds of things if I reported them. All five of them said they would make my life a living hell if I told anyone."

Kara got up and went to her sister and hugged her tight, fighting back her own tears. "Oh, Marti. I'm so sorry they did that to you. I am so sorry."

Marti released a flood of tears while Kara held her. Kara wondered if this was the first time her sister had allowed herself to cry.

Moments later Marti said, "When they left that morning for breakfast and to play basketball, I cleaned myself up and left. I went back to my own apartment and packed. I flew home to San Francisco that night."

"Did you tell the folks?"

Marti shook her head. "No. Can you imagine what Dad would have done had he known? I couldn't risk it. Mom suspected something when she saw bruises on my arms and thighs. She'd walked into my room when I was getting dressed after my shower. She'd assumed I was out by the pool with Dad and was putting more towels in my bathroom. She asked me about the bruises and I told her that I had taken a fall. But I don't think she believed me."

"So you let those guys get away with what they did to you?" Kara asked with indignation in her voice.

"Yes, because of their threats. But you know what they say about payback being a bitch. Well, I became that bitch, Kara. A few years later, all five of them eventually married, had good careers and were highly respected in the community. However, being the evil men that they were, I believed if they did it once they would do it again. So I hired a private detective to dig up what he could on them. He discovered they were involved in child pornography — they used the children of immigrants. Once we had enough evidence, we sent what we'd gathered to the state attorney's office. The five of them were arrested and convicted. And as far as I know, they're still serving time."

Kara didn't say anything as she thought about what her sister had just told her. The thought of Malcolm Edwards, the man her sister loved and thought loved her, actually raping her with his friends made her sick to her stomach. "Did they ever find out you were connected with their arrests?"

"Yes, I paid a visit to each of them individually in jail and told them they had me to thank for their current situation. It made me feel good to look into their eyes and let them know they hadn't gotten away with what they did to me. I also told them that, since they shared everything, I hoped they enjoyed sharing jail time."

Kara nodded. In a way justice had been served, but at what cost? She'd often wondered why Marti could be so cold and heartless at times when it came to men. Now she knew. But there was still one question she hadn't answered. "Why did you think Virgil would be anything like Malcolm?"

"Because he was so close to his godbrothers. They're thick as thieves, just like Malcolm and his friends were. I didn't trust them."

Kara frowned. "But you dated Xavier for almost a month."

"It was just sex. Good sex but just sex. In the end I tested him. I lied and told him I wanted marriage and that's all it took for him to drop me like a hot potato. None of those godbrothers were marriage material. I didn't think Virgil was, either. I thought he was just feeding you lies."

"Four of them are married now, Marti.

Including Xavier. So there is hope. I want to believe Virgil and I would have eventually gotten married. I loved him and I believe in my heart he loved me. I think you misjudged Virgil as well as his godbrothers. They are nothing like Malcolm and his friends."

Kara went back to her seat and looked over at her sister. "I regret what those guys did to you and I hope they rot in jail. But what you did to me and Virgil was wrong. You apologized to me but not to Virgil. I think you owe him an apology, as well."

The buzzer on Virgil's desk sounded. "Yes, Pam?"

"There's someone here to see you. A Marti Goshay."

Virgil leaned back in his chair, wondering what the hell Marti Goshay could want with him. She was the last person he wanted to see or talk to. But if she was up to something, he needed to know what. "Send her in."

"Yes, sir."

As the door opened and Marti walked in, he arched a brow. She was known to make a grand entrance whenever she walked into any room. But the woman who walked into his office looked . . . defeated. He tossed that opinion of her aside and asked, "What do you want, Marti?"

She looked everywhere other than at him. Another first. Marti was known to look any man straight in the eye and state what she wanted or didn't want. She glanced back at him. "I came to apologize for lying to Kara about you."

Her apology surprised him because he didn't think she would ever make one. Not that it mattered one way or the other now. Besides, he figured she was only apologizing to get back in Kara's good graces. "Fine. You've apologized. If there's nothing else then you can leave."

Marti turned to leave but then she turned back around. "I know I'm not one of your favorite people, Virgil. But I hope for Kara's sake the two of us can get along. What I did was wrong. I truly didn't think you loved Kara. I made a mistake. She loves you and I now know that you love her, as well. She's happy and I'm glad the two of you are back together." And then she walked out the door.

Virgil didn't say anything for a long while. Marti was wrong if she thought he loved Kara, but then, like everyone else who read *Flo on the Ro,* she assumed they'd gotten back together. That's all it was, he told himself. The gossip column made her think they were in love.

Pushing Marti's visit to the back of his mind, Virgil got back to work. He picked up the file York had overnighted to him. He was elated that he had enough goods on both Whitney and Marv Hilton. First of all, there was no way Marv could have thought Whitney was a virgin when there had been a porn video of her floating around — one that Hilton had dropped a lot of money to keep out of circulation. And Marv Hilton wasn't so clean himself. He had an expensive mistress he was trying to keep happy, not to mention his involvement in a couple of shady deals.

What the Hiltons did in their spare time was their business, but when they tried to ruin his reputation based on lies, then it became his. Leaning back in the chair he picked up the phone on his desk. "Pam, get Marv Hilton on the line."

CHAPTER 19

A smiling Virgil walked into his home later that afternoon with a bottle of champagne in his hand. Kara, who'd arrived a few minutes before, was in the kitchen. She was going to surprise him with another one of her dishes that she knew he liked — chicken and dumplings. It was another recipe his grandmother had shared with her.

"What's the occasion?" she asked, glancing at the champagne bottle he placed on the kitchen counter. Virgil pulled her into his arms.

"As usual, York came through, this time with his report on Marv Hilton as well as on Whitney. I had a conversation with Marv and told him that unless he backed off, I would send copies of what I had to the media."

"Did he agree to do it?"

"I left him no choice. He knew I meant

business and he wants to keep his secrets secret."

"Good for you."

He sniffed the air. "Mmm, something smells good."

Her smile brightened. "Chicken and dumplings. I know how much you like it."

"Yes, and I like you better," he said, leaning down for a kiss. The moment their mouths touched, she felt a rush of need travel up her spine. By the time he ended the kiss, she felt totally weak in the knees.

"I'm hungry, baby."

Her heart began pounding at his use of the endearment. It had been years since he'd called her that. "For dinner?"

"No. For you."

And then he swept her into his arms and carried her up to the bedroom.

"It's a good thing dinner was finished cooking or it would have burned by now," Kara said, sliding back into her dress.

Virgil lay there, sprawled naked on top of the covers as he watched her, feeling himself getting hard all over again. It had always been this way with her. It didn't take much for him to want her. Desire her. Lov—

He shook his head, refusing to go there. Did he need to give himself another prep talk, the same one he'd been giving himself a lot lately? The one where he swore he'd never love her again?

"Virgil?"

He blinked. "Yes?"

"You were daydreaming."

He nodded. "Yes, I guess I was. What did you say?"

A smile touched her lips. "I said don't take too long coming down. I think we can both say we worked up an appetite."

"Okay. I'll be down in a minute."

When she left he continued to lie there for a minute as he glanced around. He was just noticing the changes she'd made to his bedroom. Granted, he had moved her into his room but he hadn't expected her to take it over. It wasn't as if she was staying permanently. And where did that vase of flowers on his dresser come from? He doubted they were real but still, he never had flowers in his bedroom.

As he stood up to get dressed, a lot of crazy thoughts started flowing through his mind. What if Kara assumed she would be staying? But there was no way he could have given her that idea. Things were good between them and he enjoyed having her around, but he'd always known that in two weeks she would be gone. So had she.

Come to think of it, her two weeks were up in a few days. Then he realized something. She'd stopped giving him updates on the progress of her floors. Why?

Picking up his clothes off the floor, he went over to the closet to hang up his suit. The first thing he noticed was Kara's clothes next to his. Had they always been there? If so, then why was he just noticing them? And why was he beginning to feel crowded as though she was invading his space?

He pulled a pair of jeans off a hanger and slid them on when he heard his phone ring. Moving to the nightstand, he picked it up, knowing the caller was Uriel. "Yes, U?"

"Hey, Ellie is getting the last-minute details for my birthday party together and I need to —"

"Hey, wait a minute. I thought it was supposed to be a surprise."

Uriel laughed. "Man, you know it's hard for anyone to surprise me, especially my wife. Anyway, she wanted to know if you were bringing a guest."

Virgil frowned. "A guest? You know I always come alone. Why would you think I'd bring someone?"

"Well, you do have a houseguest."

"Who will be gone by the time your party comes around, trust me."

"Oh."

Virgil knew the sound of that "oh" and what it meant. "All right, Uriel, get it out because I know there's something you want to say."

"I just thought things were going good between you and Kara."

"They are, considering how I felt about her this time last year. I've moved her to my 'friends' category."

"Can you do that?"

Virgil raised a brow. "Do what?"

"Just be friends with a woman you used to love?"

"I don't see why not not. Like I've told you a number of times, I can't love a person who doesn't trust me."

"And like I told you, you need to let it go."

"I have."

"Not if you're still feeling that way. I hope you open your eyes before it's too late."

Kara was placing the last platter of food on the table when Virgil walked in. She smiled over at him. "You're right on time."

He sat down at the table and she immediately picked up on a change in his mood. Had something happened since she'd left him in the bedroom? He had arrived home in a festive mood and their lovemaking was, as usual, off the charts. Afterward, he had held her as he told her about his conversation with Marv Hilton.

She couldn't help wondering if anything was wrong. So she asked him. "Virgil, is everything okay?"

For some reason she felt the smile he gave her didn't quite reach his eyes when he said, "Yes, everything is fine." Then he took a seat at the table and uncovered the platters. "Everything looks good and smells delicious. Let's eat."

Over dinner she told him how her day had gone and the new clients she'd taken on. She also mentioned the article about them that morning in *Flo on the Ro.* He brought up the charity 5k walk that he was participating in next weekend and she told him she would be participating in it, as well. She suggested they walk together, but when he didn't agree right away she let it go.

For a brief moment things got quiet and when they began talking again, she couldn't help noticing he only contributed to the conversation when asked, otherwise she did most of the talking. Till after dinner, when they were doing the dishes.

"You haven't mentioned anything lately about how things are going with your floors.

They should almost be finished, right?" he asked, handing her a plate he'd just rinsed off.

For some reason, she didn't think he was asking her that for conversational purposes. She arranged the plate in the dishwasher and looked up at him. "I got a call from my contractor today, in fact. They finished early."

"It's all done?"

"Yes."

He nodded. "I don't have a problem taking off Thursday to help you move back to your place."

Kara's breath caught in her chest. "You trying to get rid of me, Virgil?"

"No, just making sure we stick to our agreement that your stay here was only temporary."

She drew in a deep breath. "But I thought . . ."

When she didn't finish what she was saying, Virgil prompted her. "You thought what, Kara?"

Kara didn't want to make a fool of herself, but she honestly thought they had been making strides in their relationship. They enjoyed being together. It was just like old times. "I thought," she said slowly, wanting to choose her words carefully, "that we'd moved beyond all the animosity."

"We have."

"Then why can't you . . ."

Again she wasn't able to get the words out. But it seemed he had no problem filling in the blanks for her. "Fall in love with you again?"

He leaned back against the counter with his hands shoved into his pockets. The man she loved with all her heart. The man she'd been convinced loved her back — she'd thought that all it would take was them spending quality time together to relive the memories. Had she been wrong?

"I told you, Kara. I could never love anyone who doesn't trust me."

Kara felt her heart breaking. He hadn't moved on. He couldn't move on. He didn't love her anymore and probably never would again. "I see."

"I hope you really do see it, Kara, because I don't want to hurt you and I refuse to lead you on by making you think there could ever be something between us again."

"But I don't understand. The time we've been spending together, our lovemaking . . ."

He didn't say anything, but in a way he didn't have to. The answer was written all over his face. To him it had been nothing more than sex.

She knew at that moment she had to leave. She refused to break down in front of him. "I think it's best if I go."

"Go where?"

Anyplace but here, she thought, moving toward the stairs. "Home. Don't worry about helping me move my stuff on Thursday. By the time you get home from work all traces of me will be gone." And then she rushed up the stairs.

Virgil stood at the window in his office and looked out. It was hard to believe it was September already and Monday would be Labor Day. He looked forward to the long weekend. *Doing what?*

One thing he could do this weekend was to celebrate. That call he'd gotten an hour ago from the Nelson Group should have him on top of the world. The deal had been finalized.

He walked back to his desk and sat down as his thoughts shifted to Kara. Returning home was for the best for her. That's what he wanted. She had started taking over the place and everybody knew he preferred his space. Women didn't spend the night at his place and they sure didn't stay for days, weeks. He'd made her an exception because of their past history but there had been no reason for her to stay any longer.

Then why was he feeling like crap?

He looked up at the knock on the door. "Come in."

His father walked in, smiling. "I just heard the news." He paused and studied his son. "For a man who just landed the company one of our biggest deals yet, you don't seem happy. You should be celebrating. Go home and take Kara someplace nice. You deserve it."

He met his father's gaze. "Kara is no longer staying at my place."

"Oh, where did she go?"

"Back home."

His father frowned. "Why?"

Virgil leaned back in his chair. "Because that's where she lives. She was only with me temporarily until her floors were done."

"Yes, I know, but your mom and I had hoped . . ."

Virgil arched a brow. "Had hoped what?"

His father met his gaze directly. "That you would finally come to your senses."

"Come to my senses about what?"

"About what Kara means to you."

Virgil shook his head. Initially when he'd suspected his father's motives for hiring Kara, he'd dismissed them. But now . . .

"Dad, can I ask you something? And I want a truthful answer."

"What?"

"Did you have ulterior motives when you hired Kara to clean up my image?"

"Yes."

"Why?"

"Because your mother and I could see what you refused to see. You're in love with the girl. And the only reason you returned to your womanizing ways was because that was your attempt to forget her. To prove to yourself you didn't need her. That you didn't love her."

Virgil stared at his father. "How could you and Mom even think that?"

"Like I said, Virgil. We saw what you refused to. Besides, I know firsthand how a lie can tear two people apart. It happened that way with Maurice."

"Who's Maurice?"

"Maurice Grant. He's a childhood friend of mine in Houston. He has a daughter named Gina and a son, Trevor. Trevor's an ex-Marine."

Virgil nodded. It had been years but he recalled Mr. Grant. He remembered that Mr. Grant would bring Gina and Trevor around whenever his family took vacations to Houston when Virgil was a kid. He also recalled that Trevor and Gina were a few years older than him and Leigh.

"Yes, what about Mr. Grant?"

"Maurice and his wife, Stella, broke up over some woman's lie and they were apart for nearly twenty years. They were able to put the past behind them a few years ago and move on. But all those wasted years. To see Maurice and Stella together now, you wouldn't think they'd spent any time apart."

Virgil shook his head. He was getting sick and tired of people thinking he should be in love with Kara. Didn't they understand how he felt? "And your point, Dad?"

His father stared hard at him. "My point, Virgil Matthew Bougard, is that I don't want it to take twenty years for you to realize that Kara Goshay is the best thing that's ever happened to you." With that, he turned and walked out.

Kara left work and walked quickly to her car. Not because she was in hurry to get home but mainly because she wasn't sure she would be able to hold it together much longer. It had been a struggle remaining at work with a broken heart.

She had been so certain of her abilities, so hyped in the belief that Virgil still loved her. That all she had to do was spend time with him to rekindle what used to be. But in less than ten minutes he had squashed that notion and destroyed all her hope.

But there was one thing about Kara Goshay that couldn't be destroyed. Her ability to survive. She had survived four years ago when she'd thought Virgil had betrayed her and her world had come to an end. It hadn't and she'd moved on. And although she was hurting inside, she was determined to survive once more.

She knew she had to spend time with him since he was still her client. Although Marv Hilton was off his back, the business agreement between her and Virgil was for them to pretend an affair for six months. Now she knew where she stood and where she would never stand again. Namely by his side.

She had gotten into her car and buckled up her seat belt when her cell phone rang. She figured it was probably Marti, but she didn't want to talk to anyone right now, not even her sister. Since Marti shared her story with Kara, she had tried to talk Marti into getting counseling. Her sister had waved off the notion, saying it was too late, but Kara didn't agree. She felt there were issues Marti still needed to resolve so that one day she could enjoy a loving relationship with a man.

Kara figured she was a good one to talk when she didn't have that kind of relationship for herself. What was more pathetic than being in love with a man who didn't love you back? A man who couldn't forgive and let go? A man who refused to love her even though she believed that he could if he just allowed himself to do so. But he wouldn't and he had proven that. So now she had to move on. She'd done it before and would do it again.

She felt bad about not taking Marti's call. She hadn't spoken to her sister in a couple of days, but Kara had texted her, claiming she was extremely busy working on an important job-related project. She didn't want Marti to think something was wrong. The last thing she wanted was for her sister to know about her current situation with Virgil. Marti would blame herself for everything, and she needed to move on, as well.

Marti had shared with her that she had sought Virgil out and apologized. For her sister to do what she did and face Virgil was a start. It didn't surprise Kara that he hadn't been receptive. She knew all too well that he was not a forgiving man.

Like she'd told Virgil two days ago, today

all her stuff would be gone when he came home. It hadn't taken more than three hours that morning for her to pack up, load the car and make two trips to her place. She hadn't realized how much extra stuff she'd purchased, assuming she was there to stay.

And when she had walked out the door of his house, she hadn't looked back. Nor had she looked around to see if Flo's posse was about. At the moment she truly didn't care.

Virgil entered his home and immediately felt a sense of loss when he glanced around. True to her word, Kara had made sure any traces of her were gone. It was as if she'd never been there. The pillows she had put on his living room sofa, the green plants she'd placed by his fireplace and that rug that had been on the floor near the breakfast bar were no longer there.

Needing a beer, he headed for the refrigerator and paused when he saw she'd left his extra key on the breakfast bar. His gut clenched. Why did he suddenly feel so lonely? It wasn't as if he'd never been alone before. For him, that was the name of the game. The only reason he could think of for his melancholy mood was that, during the days she'd been there, Kara had made her presence known, not just in his kitchen, but in every single room in his house.

It had become a common thing to come home and find her here in his kitchen, standing by the stove in her bare feet, smiling when she saw him, and then crossing the room to give him a big hug. Why had that hug been so easy to get used to? Why did he feel the need for one now?

Opening the refrigerator, he pulled out a beer, popped the tab and took a swig, needing it. Lowering the can from his lips, he thought about other times, not only in this kitchen, but throughout his house . . . both recent and when they'd been together years before. He doubted there was any room where they hadn't made love. Hell, he even remembered them making out in several of the closets, so overcome with desire for each other that they couldn't even get dressed without more heated kisses.

He couldn't help smiling at those memories. Then another memory suddenly flared in his mind. The one of how she'd looked when she'd realized he was ready for her to leave and go back to her place. He felt a tightening in his gut. He had hurt her and he'd known at that moment she'd been hoping things would turn out differently between them.

In his defense, that had been her assumption, not his. But then he couldn't help but think of how things would be without her in his life. Being the professional she was, she would honor the terms of the contract between her company and his. That meant they would still be seen together around town. Nothing had really changed. If questions came up as to why she'd moved back to her home he would just say it was closer to her job, which wasn't a lie. As long as he and Kara continued to see each other on a regular basis, no one would have reason to question their relationship.

He took another swig of his beer, knowing he was wrong about that. A lot had changed. But he refused to deal with that now. He had something else on his mind that should be taking precedence. His business deal with the Nelson Group. He would be flying to Toronto next week to finalize the paperwork between him and Stan Nelson. And earlier that day Pam had reminded him of the charity 5k walk for cancer research next weekend. In a way he was looking forward to it as a way to relieve his stress.

He frowned. When had he ever been stressed? He had a feeling he was beginning to find out just how it felt.

Chapter 20

Marti looked over at her sister. "Are you sure things are okay between you and Virgil?"

Kara paused in the middle of sipping her tea. She and Marti were having lunch at the Racetrack Café. She would have chosen another place but dining here had been Marti's idea. The last thing she needed was to run into Virgil like they'd done the last time she and her sister had been here together.

It was hard to believe but it had almost been a week since she'd seen or talked to him, although he had sent her a text message a couple of days ago to let her know of his trip to Canada. She knew the only reason he'd gone to the trouble was because of the ruse of them pretending to be lovers. It wouldn't look good if she didn't know his whereabouts if someone were to ask. She figured he was probably counting the days until he would no longer have to pretend interest in her.

She forced a smile as she answered her sister's question. "I'm positive. What makes you think otherwise?"

Marti shrugged as she picked up a French fry off her plate. "He hasn't been around."

Kara lifted a brow. "How do you know that?"

"Because you haven't mentioned him. You said you moved back to your place and didn't say why, so I assumed the two of you had a disagreement or something."

Kara didn't say anything for a minute as she took another sip of her tea, knowing Marti was watching her closely. She couldn't let Marti or anyone else know her relationship with Virgil wasn't for real. Or that she'd tried winning his heart back and failed miserably. So she said, "Everything is fine, Marti. Virgil is in Toronto finalizing an important business deal."

"I'm surprised you didn't go with him."

She wasn't. Kara knew she was the last person he would have taken, even for appearances' sake. "I have a business to run here, besides I knew he would be busy most of the time."

She knew Marti still had her suspicions, but at least she hadn't asked any more questions. Kara was glad of that. Virgil had mentioned he would be back in time for the walk on Saturday and she had to prepare herself to see him again. That was one meeting she wasn't particularly looking forward to.

Virgil entered his hotel room thinking his meeting with the Nelson Group had gone off without a hitch. All the necessary papers had been signed and it was a great day for Bougard Enterprises. He had talked to his father on his way back to the hotel, and Matthew had made plans to take Rhona out to celebrate.

Speaking of celebration, Nelson had invited him out on the town, stating he knew where they could meet up with a couple of beautiful women. But Virgil hadn't been interested and had turned him down. For some reason, he wanted to be alone tonight.

Removing his jacket, he tossed it aside and that was when he noticed the bottle of champagne that had been delivered to his room. He read the card and smiled. It was from his five godbrothers. They'd known about his trip to Toronto and were happy for him. He appreciated that.

He slid down into the chair, thinking he needed a woman. But not just any woman.

He needed Kara. He'd gotten her text message that morning letting him know that, due to an impending rainstorm, Saturday's 5k walk had been postponed.

He had texted her back and thanked her for the information and she hadn't responded. There was no reason for her to have done so, but a part of him was aching and it was an ache that wouldn't go away. His eyes lit on the bottle of champagne on the coffee table. Why was he thinking about the day he'd brought champagne home to share with Kara? Champagne they'd never gotten around to drinking because she had left that evening.

She had left because he was too stubborn, too bullheaded, too damn full of himself to accept that nobody was perfect. People made mistakes, even the people you hadn't counted on making them. Sometimes those mistakes hurt. You forgave and forgot. Life moved on. No one should live in the past.

Then why was he?

Why did the thought of what he was not allowing himself to share with Kara leave an emptiness in his stomach? A hard ache in his chest and an intense longing in his heart? Closing his eyes, he thought of her — all those times she had smiled at him, made him laugh. He realized he had shared more good times with her than bad. And those good times had been the best. He smiled as he thought about them, but he couldn't help the tightening in his groin when he especially thought of their bedtime activities.

He thought of how he would make love to her, ease into her body, feel the way her muscles would clench him in possession, how her hands would stroke him with love. Love . . .

Although she hadn't said it, he believed she still loved him. And Marti believed it, too, not that he gave much credit to her opinion. Still . . .

What about him? He'd wanted to believe all there was between them was sex. He'd held on to that conviction steadfastly . . . till now. Now he knew it had been more than that. He had only been fooling himself by claiming there was no emotional component to their lovemaking. Now was the time to admit the truth. He was in love with her.

He opened his eyes as he remembered his father's words. *My point, Virgil Matthew Bougard, is that I don't want it to take twenty years for you to realize that Kara Goshay is the best thing that's ever happened to you.*

Virgil drew in a deep breath. His father was right. She was best thing to ever happen to him. A deep sensation stirred in his gut when he remembered the pain he'd seen in her eyes the day she had left his home. Pain he had caused when he'd allowed her to believe it had only been sex between them. Now he had to convince her otherwise. He had to prove to Kara that he loved her.

He wanted to go back to Charlotte and not only tell her but show her what she meant to him. Then after spending time together rekindling what they once had and never lost, he wanted them to plan their future. He wanted to offer what he'd planned the last time. Marriage. He wanted Kara as his wife.

It didn't bother him that in making that happen he would no longer be a bachelor. He hoped Zion would understand since that would make him the lone bachelor in the club. But he figured Z could handle it.

But what he himself couldn't handle was not having Kara be a permanent part of his life. Now he understood how U, W, X and Y felt about the women they'd married. Now, more than anything, he wanted to be included in that group.

Standing, he headed toward the bathroom to take a shower and to plan. He would do whatever he had to do in order to make sure he was no longer a man who held a grudge. He was no longer a bachelor who couldn't forgive.

The forecasters had been right, Kara thought, glancing out the window. She'd awoken to the sound of pouring rain and it was still going strong. She wondered if it would lighten up any. Not that she had anywhere to go, which was why it was close to noon and she was still in her PJs. She intended to make this a lazy weekend. She'd downloaded a new book on her e-reader and, if she finished the novel in record time, she would check out a flick on the movie channel.

She refused to think about Virgil. Unless his plans had changed, he should have gotten back into town last night. Now that the walk was postponed, he had no reason to call or text to let her know. They didn't have that kind of relationship. He'd made that clear.

An hour later, after eating a grilled cheese sandwich for lunch, she was about to settle on her couch with her e-reader when she heard her doorbell. Who would be visiting her in this weather? As much as she loved her sister, she didn't need Marti right now. She had a feeling her sister still suspected something was up and that Kara wasn't being completely honest with her about her relationship with Virgil.

Easing off the sofa, Kara padded in her bare feet toward the door, loving the feel of her new floor beneath her feet. She tightened her bathrobe around her waist the minute she glanced through the peep hole. Her breath caught when she saw it was Virgil.

What was he doing here? The obvious answer came to mind and that fired her anger. Did he think it was still the status quo between them? That he could practically ignore her for over a week then show up on her doorstep for a booty call?

Snatching open the door, she glared at him. "What are you doing here, Virgil?"

"May I come in, Kara?"

She noticed then that he was wet. Rain water was dripping off him. "Yes," she said, moving aside.

Virgil paused to take off his shoes as well as his wet jacket, which he tossed across a chair on her covered porch. "Do you have a towel? I don't want to mess up your new floors," Virgil asked, not entering her home.

"Okay. I'll be right back."

Virgil stood there and watched as Kara

walked off. That gave him a chance to pull himself together. How could he not have known he still loved her? And that no matter what happened in the past he was ready to move forward? The thought of not having her in his life was something he couldn't accept. He wouldn't accept.

"Here you are."

She had returned and was handing him several thick towels. "Thanks."

He dried himself off while holding her gaze. He could feel the sexual chemistry flowing between them. He also detected something else. Love. He doubted if she could feel it yet because she was returning his stare with apprehension in her gaze.

It was only after he felt he'd sufficiently dried himself off that he crossed over her threshold, handing the towels back to her as he closed the door. When she walked off to take the towels to her laundry room, he looked around at her floors. The workers had done a nice job.

She returned and saw him still standing in the foyer. "You still haven't said why you're here, Virgil."

"I hope we can talk."

She rolled her eyes. "Talk? Yeah, right."

"You don't believe me?"

"Should I? When have you ever come here

to just talk?"

Come to think of it, he couldn't recall a time he hadn't come here with sex on his mind. "Well, this time I only want to talk."

"About what, Virgil? What could we possibly have to talk about? I think you've made it clear — you accept my apology but will never forget how I didn't trust you. That you feel there can never be love without trust. I get that. I believe you're wrong but what you think is your prerogative. I don't care anymore."

He knew it was his fault she felt that way and it would be up to him to help her care again. He leaned against the closed door. "That might have been true then, but not now. And I think we have a lot to talk about."

He could tell from the look in her eyes she was slightly confused. "Like what?"

"Like how I've been a fool. How wrong it was to be so unforgiving. How wrong I was to deny the one thing I want and need in my life. You."

When she didn't say anything and just stared at him, he decided to keep talking, spilling his soul and speaking from his heart. "I love you, Kara. I guess you can say I always have, which is why that episode hurt me so much. I allowed the pain to harden my heart, and I vowed never to love anyone again. Problem was that I loved you too much to stop loving you."

"You said you'd forgive me but wouldn't forget," Kara said, tears misting her eyes.

"No more. I'm willing to forgive and to forget," he said, slowly walking toward her. "I don't want to live in the past anymore, Kara. Instead I want to start planning a future with you. I want to pick up where we left off, to rebuild our lives together, to learn from our mistakes but not dwell on them."

Coming to a stop in front of her, he added, "I want us to dwell on each other." He wiped away her tears. "Will you forgive me for being such a stubborn unforgiving ass?"

She nodded. "Yes, I forgive you."

"And will you accept me as a man who loves you?"

She nodded again. "Only if you accept me as the woman who loves you."

"Oh, baby." And then he pulled her into his arms and kissed her.

Virgil tried not to let his hunger for Kara take over, but he loved her so much and he wanted her. It was a deadly combination. When she parted her lips to give his tongue entrance, his arousal went into high gear. But he knew what he had to do. He broke off the kiss.

The confused look in her eyes drove him to sweep her off her feet into his arms and head for the sofa. Sitting down, he cradled her in his lap. "I love you so much, baby. I never stopped loving you. Everybody could see it but me." He leaned down and brushed a kiss across her lips. "I don't want to lose twenty years with you."

Kara didn't know what he was talking about with the twenty years, but she didn't want them to lose any more time together, either. Nor was she exactly sure what had brought about this change in Virgil, but she didn't care. He was where he belonged, where she always wanted him to be. With her.

"Will you permanently improve my image by marrying me, Kara?"

She couldn't help but smile as happiness spread through every part of her. "Yes, I will marry you. I love you so much, Virgil."

"And I love you. Thanks for not giving up on me, baby. Thanks for loving me during those times I didn't deserve to be loved."

She could hardly believe she was hearing those words from Virgil now. She'd waited so long to hear him say I love you. She leaned up, wrapped her arms around his neck and pressed her mouth to his.

Virgil couldn't resist taking over the kiss, deepening it, tangling his tongue with hers. If he didn't pull back, he knew where things would lead and like he'd told her, he only wanted to talk. Pulling his mouth away from her moist lips, he said, "We need to finish talking."

A smile touched her lips. "I think we've said enough for now. We've said what's most important, don't you think?"

Instead of answering, he stood with her in his arms and headed straight for her bedroom.

He laid her down in the middle of her bed and began removing his shirt, but she put her hands on his to stop him.

"Let me."

He dropped his hands to his sides while Kara continued unbuttoning his shirt. "I can't believe you came out in this bad weather," she said softly as she worked the buttons.

"I came here straight from the airport."

She leaned back and met his gaze, surprised. "I thought you got back late yesterday afternoon."

"Flight was cancelled due to bad weather in Toronto. Had I gotten into town yesterday as planned, I would have come here before going home. Like I did today. I needed to see you just that bad."

Those words coming from him meant all the world to Kara. "When did you realize you loved me?"

"After you moved out. My house felt so lonely. And then while I was in Canada, I missed you like crazy and the more I thought about you, the more I knew."

She was going to ask him another question, the one about his twenty-year statement. But when she pushed the shirt from his shoulders and saw his hard-muscled chest, she couldn't say anything. His chest always was a turn-on for her. She liked touching it, running her fingers through the thatch of curly hair covering it. She looked down and saw how the hair tapered to a thin line as it trailed beneath the waistband of his jeans.

She looked up at him. "Remove your jeans, please."

He stepped back and did as she'd asked, dragging the jeans slowly down his hips and muscular thighs, knowing she was watching him. He did the same with his briefs. Her heart picked up a beat when she gazed upon his engorged sex. Just thinking about what it would do to her, imagining the feel of it sliding in and out of her, sent heated sensations rushing all through her. Virgil Bougard was such a masculine man and seeing him naked made her appreciate being a woman. The woman he loved. The woman who loved him in return.

At that moment she couldn't help saying the words again. "I love you."

He smiled and cupped her cheek, meeting her gaze. "And I love you. I intend to spend the rest of my days showing you how much and how deeply."

Virgil then joined her on the bed. Skimming his hands down below her waist to the area between her legs, he felt her hot and ready. That was good because he was more than ready for her. All through the flight back to Charlotte, he'd thought of nothing but professing his love for her and then making love to her. Now that he was here, beside her, his entire body quivered in anticipation.

Positioning his body over hers, he glanced down at her and said the words he'd held back from saying all the times they'd made love this past month. "I love you, Kara."

He lowered his head to kiss her at the same exact moment he slid inside of her. He deepened the kiss as he began moving, thrusting in and out of her, setting into motion a rhythm that had her digging her fingers into his shoulders. But he was too far gone to feel any pain. The sensation of her inner muscles clenching him made him break off the kiss and close his eyes and moan.

No woman had ever made him feel like this. As though he was ready to blast off to parts unknown, a galaxy not yet discovered. One that only Kara could take him to in a blaze of heat and desire. He felt his insides trembling, and when she arched her body and opened her thighs just a little wider, he convulsed in pleasure.

A growl of deep satisfaction escaped his throat as his body was wracked with intense spasms. When she screamed his name, he knew she had joined him over the edge. Perfect. She once said no one was perfect. Well, he had news for her. She was.

Years ago she had done something no other woman had done and that was getting him to fall in love with her. Not with manipulations, deceptions or schemes. She had made it clear that she would not let him or any man compromise her principles. Lord knows he'd tried. But in the end she had won him over and he'd fallen head over heels in love with her. And he would love her until the day he died.

Kara snuggled close to Virgil after having

thoroughly been made love to. She felt his arms tighten around her as if he never intended to let her go. She had no problem with that because she never intended to let him go, either.

She heard his even breathing and for a minute she thought he'd dozed off, until he leaned over and placed a kiss on the side of her face. "I love you," he whispered close to her ear. "And I intend to say it every chance I get."

Kara shifted her body to look up at him and smiled. "I definitely don't have a problem with that." She paused a moment then said, "Now tell me what you meant earlier about twenty years."

He told her about his conversation with his father, about his dad's childhood friend Maurice Grant.

Kara sat up in bed and looked down at him. "Let me get this straight. Your father had ulterior motives for hiring me?"

"Yes. Granted, my image did need improving and you're the best in the field, but I believe that I could have handled things my way. York was already on it."

Kara was so filled with love for Virgil. They'd been given another chance at love and she knew moving forward their love would only get stronger.

He pulled her into his arms and captured her mouth in a long and drugging kiss. When he released her mouth, he said, "This is the perfect weather to eat, sleep and make love."

Kara snuggled closer to Virgil, thinking that she definitely agreed.

EPILOGUE

"Welcome to our home and congratulations," Ellie Lassiter said with her husband, Uriel, by her side. "And I love your ring. It's beautiful."

"Thanks." Kara couldn't help glancing down at her engagement ring. The one Virgil had slid on her finger two nights ago. It was a Zion exclusive and she thought it was beautiful, too.

"Have the two of you decided on a wedding date?" Uriel asked, grinning.

"In March. That gives you and the other godbrothers six months to clear your calendars," Virgil said, pulling Kara closer to his side.

Virgil's parents had been ecstatic when they were told of their engagement. Her parents had been overjoyed, as well. Marti — who had finally confided to her parents what Malcolm had done years ago, had entered counseling and was doing well —

had agreed to be Kara's maid of honor. Kara had told Virgil what had happened to Marti and she'd appreciated his understanding in her wanting to rebuild a relationship with her sister. Florence Asbury had been thrilled to get the exclusive about the engagement for her *Flo on the Ro* column.

An hour later Kara decided she liked all the wives of the four married bachelors as well as Virgil's five godfathers and their wives. Most of them she remembered from the last time she and Virgil had dated. All of them were still married except for Uriel's parents. They had gotten a divorce.

"I wonder where Carolyn's boy-toy is tonight. She looks out of place without him," Virgil said.

"What do you mean?"

Virgil then told Kara how, after over thirty years of marriage, Carolyn Lassiter had shocked her husband and son when she announced she didn't want to be married anymore and had begun seeing a man twenty-six years her junior.

From the looks of things, Kara thought Carolyn Lassiter might be regretting those actions. Kara noticed how every so often Carolyn would glance over at her ex-husband and the beautiful woman by his side. According to Virgil, Anthony had begun dating the widowed Claire Steele, the aunt to Mayor Morgan Steele, around three years ago. She was an extremely beautiful woman. When she stood with her daughters — Vanessa, Taylor and Cheyenne — she could pass for their sister. Like her youngest daughter Cheyenne, Claire's Native American features — the dark eyes, high cheekbones and straight black hair — gave her a distinguished look.

"May I have everyone's attention?"

Kara turned to see Anthony Lassiter stand in the middle of the room.

"He's probably about to toast Uriel for his birthday," Virgil said as he leaned over to her.

"Before I toast the birthday boy," Anthony said with a grin. "who I think is the best son any man could have, I want to acknowledge that another one of my godsons will be getting married in six months, and I just want to say, Virgil, all your godfathers are proud of you. And, Kara, welcome to the family."

They accepted the applause and Kara could hardly believe her good fortune. She had to look down at her shiny new ring again to believe she'd actually become Virgil's fiancée.

Anthony then glanced around, spotted

Zion across the room and chuckled. "You can't be in that club by yourself, Zion."

Zion laughed. "Want to bet?"

That caused everyone to burst into laughter. It seemed Zion Blackstone had no problem being the lone bachelor in the Guarded Hearts Club. The last bachelor.

Then, while everyone watched, Anthony reached out his hand and Claire joined him. "I'm happy to tell you that we've decided to take our relationship to another level, and with the blessings of my son and Claire's daughters, we've decided to marry. It will be a Thanksgiving wedding. We felt that day was appropriate since the two of us have a lot to be thankful for."

When he leaned over and kissed Claire on the lips, everyone clapped and cheered. Everyone except for Anthony's ex-wife, Carolyn. Kara wondered if she was the only one who noticed the regret in Carolyn's eyes before she slipped off to the ladies' room.

Before anyone could approach the couple to offer more congratulations, another godfather took center stage. This time it was Matthew.

"May I have everyone's attention?"

The noise level lowered as a beaming Matthew held up his hands. "You aren't the only one with good news to share, Anthony. I just want to announce that as of January first, I will be officially retiring from Bougard Enterprises and leaving the company in my son's capable hands. I know he will do well, especially since he'll have a good woman by his side."

Virgil, who hadn't known about his father's decision, was momentarily speechless. When he finally found his voice, he crossed the room to his father and gave him a bear hug. The torch had officially been passed. He then crossed the room back to Kara and pulled her into his arms. He could hardly believe the way things had worked out. He'd gotten the helm of Bougard Enterprises and, more important, the woman he loved. Overcome with emotion, he leaned down to give his future wife a kiss, not even hearing the cheers of their audience.

"I can't wait for March to get here," Virgil said later that night with Kara snuggled up close to his side.

Uriel and Ellie had put most of the attendees up for the night at their lake house. But Virgil and Kara had decided to stay at a hotel in Gatlinburg a few miles away.

"I can't wait, either," Kara said, staring up at him.

Last week they decided for Kara to move back into his home. He loved waking up with her each morning and going to bed with her at night. They had flown to California to talk to her parents and decided the wedding would take place at Kara's home in San Francisco. He and Marti were trying to build a better relationship. After all, they would be in-laws.

Unable to help himself, Virgil lowered his mouth to Kara's and began kissing her with all the love he felt in his heart.

When he finally released her mouth, she smiled up at him. "What was that for?"

"No reason. That's my way to say I love you."

She wrapped her arms round his neck. "In that case you can use that way to tell me anytime."

He chuckled. "I'm glad."

He then proceeded to kiss her again.

ABOUT THE AUTHOR

Brenda Jackson is a *New York Times* best-selling author of more than one hundred romance titles. Brenda married her childhood sweetheart, Gerald, and has two sons. She lives in Jacksonville, Florida. She divides her time between family, writing and traveling. Email Brenda at authorbrendajackson@gmail.com or visit her on her website at brendajackson.net.

The employees of Thorndike Press hope you have enjoyed this Large Print book. All our Thorndike, Wheeler, and Kennebec Large Print titles are designed for easy reading, and all our books are made to last. Other Thorndike Press Large Print books are available at your library, through selected bookstores, or directly from us.

For information about titles, please call:
   (800) 223-1244

or visit our Web site at:
   http://gale.cengage.com/thorndike

To share your comments, please write:
Publisher
Thorndike Press
10 Water St., Suite 310
Waterville, ME 04901